DEAR DIARY, IT'S ME

LUCINDA LAMONT

To anyone who is struggling with anything. You are enough.

January 3rd 2019

Dear diary, it's me.

I know we haven't spoken in a while. Ok, maybe 'a while' is putting it lightly, but I think I'm ready now. I think it's time. I'm scared, but I will always be scared until I just come out with it.

I don't feel confident, but I do feel as though I can make the leap from the edge I have been teetering on for some time now.

I don't know where to start. Ok, maybe if I just start with:

'Hi, my name is Alice. I'm a twenty-five-year-old primary school teacher and I'm ...'

But wait, what if I'm not? What if I'm making this out to be bigger than it is? Deep down I know it, but I haven't had the courage to say it out loud before or even write it down. If I say it, if I write it, will I accept it? Will I surrender to it because right now I feel like I'm fighting it. It has become a constant battle that consumes my thoughts from the minute I wake up.

I've been fighting it for about eighteen months now. I've mentioned it to a few people who have mostly laughed it off. They would dismiss it and say I was overthinking again, or that many people were the same, but you'd get the odd person who would ask for more information and then raise an eyebrow when you gave them a story that was, shall we say, played down ever so slightly.

Confession number 1 – I tell lies.

I should elaborate. They are not massive lies. Just lies that make me feel better about myself. Lies that avoid public shame but contribute to increased in-

ternal shame. For example, 'I drink a bottle of wine most nights.' The truth? I drink a bottle of wine every night. Sometimes more, but honestly, I try to limit it to that. What scares me is that I can't go less. I can't open a bottle of wine and not finish it. The first glass takes the edge off the night before and settles the anxiety that was caused by said stupid poison (see, I know it's poison and I know it's stupid, but I still want it). 'Second-Glass Alice' is up for some fun and suddenly enjoying the day at this point more than any minute previous to it. The second glass is much more enjoyable than the first and brings my personality to life. 'Third-Glass Alice' is a different Alice again. The third glass makes me feel sad and thinking about texting him and wondering why he is not texting me and then finally, Alice needs the fourth glass to knock her out and make her go to sleep.

I have on occasion tried to buy a couple of beers because I don't like beer. I drink them and then walk— ok, cue shame—maybe drive to the garage and buy a bottle of wine and drink the whole lot, and you can only guess what tomorrow's Alice is going to need to feel ok about it all again? Yup, more wine.

Ok, let's try again. Hi. I am Alice. I am twenty-five years old and I'm ... God, why is this so hard? Just say it, Alice. Once it's out there, you can live a more honest life.

I think for a moment. I step up from my desk and walk in a circle around my bedroom, hands on hips, and biting my bottom lip.

Are you sure about this, Alice?

'Oh, fuck off,' I retort at the bully living inside my head.

Once again, I sit back at my laptop and begin writing again.

I am trying to tell you that I think ... I think I'm an alcoholic. Possibly a high-functioning one. That's the first step.

My head goes tingly with the confession, as though I can feel particles of relief exiting my body and immediately I feel slightly brighter. I feel empowered suddenly and pull the laptop closer to me and being typing furiously away.

Where do you want me to start? My story is no different from anyone else's. I was allowed the odd drink at family gatherings as a young teenager but by the age of eighteen, I was regularly getting absolutely smashed. I was the loudest, the wildest ... had to drink more than anyone, had to have that extra shot, had to be one of the lads, had to be at the centre of anything. I was raucous. A hoot. The entertainment. Then, the morning would come. I would be devastated when I would hear rumours of people claiming I was attention-seeking and full of myself. I actually wasn't. I was trying desperately to fit in. To feel ok in my own skin—when I didn't.

#Confession of an alcohol dependant number 2 – We are not comfortable in our own skin.

How did that happen? I was a smart girl. I had lots of friends at school. I was into sports. Then, I hit fifteen and started smoking and drinking. I gave up taking care of myself and did what all, no, most of my friends were doing. Living for the weekend. Over the years that followed I became insecure, shy in a group, jealous, untrusting, bitchy, paranoid, and worst of all? Ignorant. Now I'm twenty-five with a decent enough job, drinking a bottle of wine every night, but worse than that, thinking about drinking from the moment I wake up until 5.00 P.M. Sometimes, 4.30 P.M. Ok, sometimes a glass of wine with lunch. And that's what makes me in control, right? Wrong.

#Confession of an alcohol dependant number 3 – I am concerned about how much I think about alcohol.

I know what you're thinking. One bottle of wine a night is not an out-of-control alcoholic. I know that. I go to work. I pay my bills. I wash and iron my clothes and keep a clean house.

What if all of the things that aren't going brilliantly for me are a direct result of my alcohol abuse?

Allow me to clarify.

- *I don't trust anyone.*
- *I don't think I'm attractive.*
- *I don't think I'm clever.*
- *I don't feel like I fit in anywhere.*
- *I yo-yo from crippling anxiety to not giving a damn about anything.*
- *I feel disconnected.*
- *I can't concentrate.*
- *I have memory problems.*
- *I have mood swings.*
- *I feel grey, as if I am in a constant lull.*
- *I used to be happy.*
- *I'm bored of my job.*
- *I am in an unhappy relationship.*
- *I have an opinion, usually controversial, on pretty much everything.*
- *I am definitely not easy-going.*

What if I am not any of the above? What if my time spent poisoning my brain has left me with a number of venomous passengers? There is only one way to find out. It has taken me a long time to get here, but today I begin.

My name is Alice and I'm an alcoholic.

I have decided to quit drinking. I have spent so much time analysing my own mind in recent years and coming up with reason after reason as to what could be wrong with me. I even visited the doctor and told her I thought I was bipolar. She laughed at me and told me to get some exercise and fresh air. I bought a bottle of wine instead.

My boyfriend can't do anything right. He takes me out for dinner and I get drunk and slur insults at him. I used to love being in his company and now everything he does annoys me. I blame him for all that is wrong in our relationship and I drink because it's all his fault. The strange thing is I barely drank when we met. He's not a heavy drinker and yet I have become one. I have changed so much since we met.

Work doesn't challenge me enough and I can do it with my eyes closed. The six-year-olds keep me distracted from my dull sense of reality. That's what one bottle of wine a night does to a person. I don't feel horrifically hungover, I just feel dull. Nothing is exciting. Nothing seems like fun. I should be head of year by now, but my performance has suffered due to my desire to push myself out of my comfort zone and crap sleep. Like I said, I can do the day job but I'm not exactly going above and beyond. Some of the newly qualified teachers come in bursting with ideas. Not me. I can't be arsed. Can't be arsed with anything actually. They won't promote me because I won't do more than I have to and I'm too lethargic to look elsewhere. Plus, I know I can keep drinking and manage that job. If I got a more senior role, I might have to cut down on drinking. That doesn't feel like a good option right now.

Can you see the pattern here? It's taken a long time for me to see that the fault lies within me. I used to love my job. I was ambitious and good at it. I used to love my boyfriend and he used to love me. I don't know why he's still here. Maybe because he's hoping I will snap out of it. Disclosure: he does not know how much I drink. No one does. And that there lies the truth. The truth that has led me to change. I used to go out and drink because I didn't want to be alone. Now, I sit in and drink alone because I don't want anyone to see how much I drink. You see how the once fun activity has now become a destroyer of all good things? I am on the brink of losing things that mean a lot to me and so it is time to wake up and smell the coffee.

———

Today is day one of my sobriety and I feel empowered. I have become so fed up of always feeling crap and I am learning that moderation isn't right for me at the moment. In order to reverse the addiction that I have accrued, I need to reverse what I've done.

I don't think it's going to be nice. I don't think it's going to be pretty, but I am going to take you with me. Every step of the way. You are going to help me rid myself of this horrid affliction once and for all. Dear diary, I know this isn't the type of insert you were expecting from me, but I think only you can help. Writing this to you is my confession and the beginning of change.

Good night, Alice xx

January 4th 2019

Dear diary, it's me, Alice.

I did it! I really did it! I did a whole booze-free twenty-four hours. When I went to bed last night, I felt so good. I was elated and even had a slither more confidence just for cracking that one day. I stayed up later than normal because I wasn't knocked out for once. I was able to read in bed and concentrate! I took in every word and digested it. I felt the paper between my fingers and I could smell the scent of the pages. I love the smell of books. They remind me of a time before the digital age. Long live the book! I read, and I read some more. Something I haven't done for a long time. Oh, and another thing. I watched a crime documentary on Netflix and I remembered it in detail this morning. I feel so proud of myself!

When I woke up, my glass of water on the side table was untouched. I was hydrated enough, so it seems. No more knocking it over in the middle of the night because I'm pissed!

I slept like a log. I didn't get up needing a wee. Another bonus. It's only the first day and I am reaping the benefits already.

That makes me feel a pang of shame and almost immediately I think about alcohol to subdue any feelings of guilt. No. I snap my mind shut, away from the obtrusive thoughts creeping in.

I got on with my day and achieved so much. I completed all my tasks at work that I had to do. My colleagues and boss all waved goodbye to me in the car park as we left the school for the day. I hadn't sneaked out, avoiding eye contact with them as had become the norm. There was actual joy in the staffroom at lunchtime today. Compliments exchanged as coffees were being made, smiles and thanks as biscuits were passed round. It wasn't the hellhole I had allowed it to become in my mind. There are decent people there who hungover me had completely disregarded.

I was more helpful than usual and kinder to my colleagues. I had a spring in my step. Some of them looked suspicious and I think I heard some of them whispering about me as I heated up my jacket potato. They were probably shocked to see me eating something that wasn't greasy. I don't care and if anything, it is to be expected. They won't have been whispering about what I did at the last office party. They would have been whispering about the new and improved me, and that's the kind of whispering I am happy about.

I did think about alcohol from about 11 A.M. onwards. It wasn't a craving as such; it was the bully inside my head telling me I wouldn't make it and that I should pick up a bottle on the way home. It was telling me that I mess everything up, that's just me, it's who I am, and that alcohol takes the pain away. Then it occurred to me. I started out using alcohol to take away social anxiety pains and now I need alcohol to take away alcohol pains. Huh, never saw that one coming when I was a teenager full of hope and completely ignorant to excessive alcohol consumption!

By the time the evening came, and I had shrugged off the day, my buzz has worn off slightly and I am feeling a little down if I'm honest. I am writing to you to distract my thoughts and to remind myself, or engrain in my brain, that alcohol is not my friend. It takes away way more than it gives. It steals from tomorrow. I know the evenings are going to be hard so now that you've been updated, I'm going to go and light some candles, run a bath, and find an empowering audio book to listen to.

Oh, and diary, we made it through day two.

Thanks, Alice xx

January 5th 2019

Dear diary, it's me.

Today has been weird. I don't feel as elated as I have been the last two days. I'm wondering if I always need to achieve something. Once I've achieved it, it doesn't seem fun anymore. Maybe Dan has a point. He says I am never satisfied, that I can't sit still, and maybe that's where it is going wrong with Dan and me. Let's cover that later. Right now, we are still at the sobriety gate.

I feel good. I still feel like I am kind of achieving something but that insatiable buzz from the first twenty-four hours has gone. Don't worry; it hasn't gone entirely. I am still focused. If there is one thing I can tell you, it's that 'Day-Three Alice' is examining 'Drinking Alice' a lot more and it is food for thought. I don't want to make any promises yet, but I can already see that a life without booze is a life worth living. A life with booze is so restricted. Before, I used to think that nothing would be fun without alcohol. I used to snigger at sober people before, thinking that they were bores, socially inept and all-round losers. Sober Alice is beginning to see how wrong I was and how much more you can have in one day (let alone a life) by cutting out boozing. I am getting on and doing things. I am not putting anything off. I am cramming in activity after activity because I can and because I want to. I feel like the personality that I gradually lost is slowly creeping back in.

Today, I was driving in my car and I sang along to nearly every song. I tapped my fingers on the wheel. I let other cars have the right of way. I smiled whilst queuing at traffic lights and felt like the green light didn't just mean go for the cars, it felt like green meant go just for me. I feel like I am aligning with the universe. I am definitely happier, kinder, and more patient. A couple of times I cursed other road users and found myself correcting my bad attitude straight after. I am only human after all. Small steps, diary. Small steps.

Before I close for the night, I'm hungrier. I'm aware of so much at the moment now that I am not dulling down my brain every day, and another thing I have found is that I enjoy food. The sugar cravings seem to have subsided slightly, but I could eat more, and food is tasting great. I used to eat to sober up or soak it up. It was never to savour the moment or to enjoy fine cuisine. It was medicinal. Today, I made a toasted pitta with mayonnaise and sliced cucumber and tomatoes. Not exactly award winning I know, but it was heavenly. The juices were so refreshing and felt like moisturiser for my internally ravaged body.

I might not be as buzzing today as I was yesterday or the day before, but it's a time of reflection. I know I am happier, but for some reason today, fear is lingering. Fear as in I'm not sure if I completely trust myself to stick at this, but I am determined to try. People often think a breakthrough is a beautiful thing. I think things have to get pretty ugly before the sun can shine.

Good night diary.

Thanks for listening. Alice xx

January 7th 2019

Dear diary, it's me.

Sorry I didn't write in you yesterday. I took the day off from thinking and talking and had a day of doing. Another plus on the 'not drinking' list. I felt much more upbeat than I had the day before. Perhaps day three was just a flop day. I did give it a bit of thought and realised I need to accept that I am not going to feel wonderful every day. I guess, if I'm being honest, I kinda hoped I would feel amazing every day. I mean, I have been feeling crappy for ages and told myself it was the booze, but then I used the booze to make me feel not crappy. I know I am definitely brighter for not drinking, but I was a tad dismayed to feel a bit lack-lustre on day three. I have reminded myself that none of us live in sheer delight every day on God's green earth. We have got to learn to accept that some days are just a bit shit for no reason. No amount of green tea or healthy eating or yoga (spoiler alert, I don't do yoga) will guarantee you a fabulous day. Sure, it helps, but sometimes we just feel shit and you know what won't help? Drinking.

I have come up with a new mantra that I thought I would share with you too. I am still thinking about al-cohol a lot across the day. Maybe not quite as much as day one, but still more than I'd like to. I think about socialising, about weddings, birthdays, dinners, and how I think I would struggle to not be able to join in. So, with that in mind my new mantra is: you only have to say no today. That seems much more achievable. I need to stop looking into the future and take this one day at a time and the great news is, if I ask myself, do I want a drink now? The answer is no, because I only have to say no today. It seems to be working for me. A bit like when you get prescribed antibiotics and you're not allowed to drink whilst taking them. It's easy because you know it's not forever. So, I can stop drinking. I only have to say no today.

I went and spent the night with Dan last night. I am disconcerted to find that I still do not enjoy his company, even now sober. I just feel prickly around him. Like, he can't do anything right. The guy cannot do a thing without annoying me. Maybe he can't do right because I can't forgive him for being wronged. I admire people that can walk away when they have been betrayed. When they 'know their worth.' I do know my worth and it broke my heart and made me want to fight for my place. To fight for the love that belonged to me. I don't know. I will give it a bit longer, but I am realising that I am happier on my own than spending time with him and I'm pretty sure he feels the same. It's just none of us have the guts to pull the plug—yet. It's like we don't want each other but we don't want us to be with anyone else either. We are just going through the motions, I guess.

Basically, I went over there and dinner was ready to be served and he sat me down and put a film on. I felt like he had set up the arena for no conversation. Sure, he didn't want to talk, to ask about my day, to touch me, to hug me, or even to tell me anything interesting about his day. He wanted me to eat, shut up, watch a film, and then guess what? When the film was done, he wanted to get his end away. I ended up telling him that. He dismissed it as he always does when it's a negative comment about him. We went up to bed and I gave him what he wanted. Then it was lights out and *he rolled over and was snoring within five minutes. I took myself to his spare bedroom and slept in there. In the morning, he made me a coffee and I had a shower and left. I reckon across the whole event, I've written more words to you than we spoke to each other.*

Maybe before I declare myself an alcoholic, I should in fact make sure I am not surrounded by arseholes.

Good night, Alice xx

January 10th 2019

Dear diary, it's me.

Sorry I have been away again for a couple of days. I feel like I am dumping my feelings on you and then absconding. I feel bad, as if you're a person … it's all about me and I'm not asking how you are, but right now you are my most loyal friend.

It's been a busy couple of days. I am still not drinking. I am at the point where I don't even want it. I'm still thinking about it more than I want to and it's as if the alcohol parasite within me is getting annoyed that I am not feeding it. It seems as if the thoughts are getting nastier before they get easier. I imagine him / her / it to be like a piece of paper dancing in a fire. You know when you crumple up a piece of paper and chuck it on an open fire? At first, the edges slowly take light, that was like the first few days of sobriety, and then finally the whole piece is on fire before turning to ash. I think that's where we are at, and the defeated ash is imminent.

I keep thinking I miss it and I still don't know if this is a temporary pledge or a permanent one; all I know is that I am going to keep saying no.

Music is still sounding great and food … oh my God. Food is blowing my mind. The flavours! The smell. I can't believe how much gets watered down by excessive alcohol consumption. It's not just the mind that it dulls, it seems to dull all the senses.

Another thing I have noticed, and this is an advance warning for tmi (too much information), my pms has not been nearly as bad this month. I feel mildly agitated whereas in previous months, I was *fuming and ready for battle for a week before I was due. Now, I feel positively calm and in control. Is that balanced hormones or does it come from being in control? Either way, another positive.*

I thought seeing as I keep rambling on to you about my progress, maybe I should actually make a list.

The pros and cons of alcohol:
Pros:

- *Quietens my mind (*during the period of consumption).*

Cons:

- *It dulls my senses.*
- *Makes me depressed.*
- *Makes me send text messages I don't mean.*
- *Affects my sleep.*
- *Stops me from being productive.*
- *Creates hangovers.*
- *Makes me moody.*
- *Makes me impatient.*

That's just off the top of my head.
The pros and cons of sobriety:
Cons:

- *Not everyone gets it.*

Pros:

- *I feel happy again.*

- *I feel kinder.*
- *I feel more patient.*
- *I feel creative.*
- *I am saving money.*
- *I am sleeping better.*
- *I am reading more.*
- *I am remembering more.*
- *I am not embarrassing myself.*
- *I am not degrading myself.*
- *My self - respect is returning.*
- *I am enjoying music again.*
- *I have signed up for an art class.*
- *I dumped Dan.*

I suppose I had better tell you about that. I know I said I would give it more time but being sober is giving me a new sense of clarity. After spending the night there two nights ago and coming away feeling like something he could've ordered online, I felt enough was enough. I want to be greeted at the door with a kiss and a cuddle. I want him to take my coat and ask me how my day was, maybe tell me my hair smells good. I wanted him to tell me about what he's been up to that day. I wanted to snuggle on the sofa. I wanted us to stroke each other as we watched the film. I wanted to touch. I wanted us to talk after the film ended, ex-change thoughts. I wanted him to chase me up the stairs and smack my bum playfully. I wanted him to get into bed and whisper sweet nothings to me and kiss me. I do not want to go to bed in silence and him get into it wearing a hard-on and nothing else.

He doesn't make me feel good. He makes me feel worthless. There are people out drinking in every bar known to man who would be happy to have no strings sex and never speak again. Go and get one, Dan. I expect more from a lover of three-plus years.

We were supposed to be fixing our relationship after his infidelity, but he isn't interested in repairing it. He just wants sex and nothing more. I feel so stupid for taking him back. I've never felt so low in my life. As you know, I have tried to end the relationship many times, but he always came crawling back, promising the stuff that dreams are made of, and I suppose I fell for it because I wanted to know he wanted me more than her. The truth is, he wants whatever he can get and through discovering that conclusion, I have walked around with my broken heart in a glass jar that he then kicked down a cobbled street whilst skipping and whistling all the while and dangling the proverbial carrot of happy-ever-after.

I will never be happy with him. I don't think you can ever be happy with someone again once they insert themselves into another whilst supposedly being in love with you. I should've walked then. I think I needed to exhaust it until I didn't love him anymore. I was worried that if I walked and he met someone else and was happy, I would resent what was left for me. Now, I know he is incapable of love and loyalty and that I should feel sorry for whoever he ends up with next. If I leave now, I get another chance at finding my dream. If I stay with him I will never live in wedded bliss, I will live with crippling insecurities. I am better than that. I am worthy of being loved. I am enough for one man. I am pretty. I am clever, and I will not let his disdain for women define me.

I am walking dear diary, and I'm sticking to it.

Love, Alice xx

January 14th 2019

Dear diary, it's me.

Where to start? Last time we spoke, I had called things off with Dan. He doesn't seem bothered. In fact, he agreed it was for the best and said I make him miserable. I don't care and that tells me everything I need to know. We don't love each other. That's all it boils down to.

So, I ended it. It's done. However, we have been here before. I would like to think I won't get back together with him, but I have been weak more times than I care to count. I think I have crawled back because I want his validation. I've learned that what I need is to get some respect. Self-respect. At the end of the day, if a guy wants to be with you, he will. If he wants to text you, he will. He will do all the things he did in the beginning. I don't even recognise Dan now. He is not a smidge of the man I met. He is a fake. It was all an act to get into my pants. The fact it is over is a good thing. The problem is I am happiest when I am in love and I miss that feeling. I want it and I thrive on it. I hope we can move on as painlessly as possible. I can't think of him being with someone else. Christ, even just giving it a second thought hurts. It will get easier. It will pass. I just need to keep busy and stay away from alcohol. Alcohol never fixes a problem, it makes the problem worse.

Anyway, that was where I was at a couple of days ago. I have continued to avoid alcohol and have continued to make observations. I have started to up my standards. I am a Sagittarius, after all. I have extremely high standards. I am picky with everything. Actually, allow me to change that. I had high standards. The alcohol consumption took those away. Another thing it took, just so that I wouldn't be lonely. I became sloppy. To the average person, I was still well turned out and my house was still clean and tidy, but I knew things were slipping. I stopped shaving my legs regularly. My eyebrows were neglected. I would wear outfits that were frumpy. The skirting boards in the house were dusty. The shower door had a layer of limescale on it. The taps needed polishing. You see? Some people don't care about those things anyway, but to me, these were jobs that normally got done. I had begun to not care, all because of alcohol. Imagine if at the start of your alcohol journey, if a prescriber gave it to you and said, 'You know that excess consumption of this will alter your personality beyond the period of consumption?' Would you still do it? Maybe. Maybe that doesn't scare you, but are you really comfortable becoming someone you're not? Becoming a version of you that nature did not intend?

Something that occurred to me this week is that if you come across someone who is mean, show them love. I became mean when the addiction was kicking in. I became mean because I was so unhappy. I now believe people who are mean and angry are actually very sad and they need our love. They are fighting a battle they are trying to keep a secret. It might not be alcoholism, but I am a firm believer no one is born mean. Life made them that way. Help them to see there is another way.

Anyway, work continues to go from strength to strength. My booze-free attitude is winning me many *points and I even got invited out for lunch by some of the other teachers this week. They said they wanted to get out of the school because we all know how exhausting and draining the long days of teaching in the winter can be. We were all willing half term to hurry up. They could've done that months ago, but they didn't want to, and I know why. Because I was a bitch. I was negative, I used to slag people off and I was unenthused. Who wants that at their lunch table? I'm glad they gave me another chance. This Alice is someone I would be happy to be friends with. I did find it slightly tricky ordering a lime and soda as they all chose alcohol, but I felt better for it. 'Everything is fine after a glass of wine!' I smiled as we all clinked glasses, grimacing inside about them believing alcohol makes things better.*

Whilst out for lunch, I got asked out by someone at the bar. I have accepted. I'm not sure if I'm ready yet. I still think about Dan a lot, but I know he doesn't want me. It crossed my mind this week that this version of me has never been out dating before. I could be about to become the best girlfriend ever, and Dan is going to miss out. He dated the old me. What if he is more compatible with the new me? That being said, his treatment of me contributed to my alcohol abuse, so perhaps he doesn't deserve the new me. Perhaps the new me deserves someone new.

Finally, I want to reveal that I have still been feeling a bit sad again. I am sad, but I am more hopeful than ever. I see this sadness as a necessary unpleasant emotion as I transition from what was familiar into something new. I'm sad at the relationship I have lost but I am eager to work with the new Alice. I know it will be ok and I definitely know that alcohol is not the way forward.

Thanks for listening diary. You're a good friend.

Love, Alice xx

January 28th 2019

Dear diary,

I have been a bad, bad girl. Stupid. Idiotic. Self-sabotaging, moronic, complete and utter twat. You know that already because I haven't written for more than two weeks. I was on such a roll.

I found the first week very easy. I felt elated, powerful, confident, and happy. The second week was much more arduous. My inner gremlin seemed to grow stronger despite me trying to beat him away by not feeding him with alcohol. Maybe it was one last insurgence before I battered him for good. You know how like when someone dies, they can suddenly take one last surprising gasp of breath? Maybe it was that, but he got me.

I was offered a promotion at work. Head of English. It completely took me by surprise and my immediate reaction was to celebrate. I had proven my point. I had been dry for two weeks, I felt that the grass was not as green as I had hoped it would be, but that I knew that I could take a break if I wanted to, and so I bought a bottle of Prosecco and drank the whole lot alone. I told myself I could return to the old me for just one night. I justified to myself that I deserved it. I had achieved success at work and that was worth some recognition. I tried to call Dan. He didn't answer, nor did he call back or send a text to ask what I wanted. I instantly regretted that move. I allowed myself one night off from my path of sobriety.

The following day, I woke up wanting more alcohol and I knew I had awoken the beast. I didn't care. I was going to go back to alcohol. I can still get pro-

moted when my life isn't perfect, and Dan still doesn't care even if I am trying to clean up my act. I felt as though, or at least convinced myself that, the universe was telling me I was beating myself up too much and once again the devil within me started his shit and I believed him.

'Everyone is doing it. You need it. You're better with it. No one cares, really. You can still function. Just have a bloody drink. Stop being so hard on yourself. Everyone drinks. Enjoy it.'

I binged for four days.

On the fourth day, I woke up feeling terrible and ashamed. I felt awful. I felt as though I'd had three times the amount I had actually had. It was time to stop. I had my fun and now it was time to clean up again. Maybe I could binge once a month, I reasoned with myself (losing the fight before I have even begun).

Then, Dan got in touch. He wanted to meet up. Said he would book a lovely hotel and take us away for an evening. I was happy. Coming out of a four-day alcohol binge, I needed some comfort. I needed to feel loved and he came knocking at exactly the right time. I don't need to be perfect. I'm allowed a drink! I am doing well at work and Dan wants me back. Things are good. Not.

As soon as we arrived, he wanted to have sex. I wasn't ready. I had hoped he could tell me he missed me and that he wanted to be with me and talk about our future. It seemed to me as if he opened the hotel room door and dropped his trousers instantaneously. I giggled as he made his moves on me because I wasn't relaxed. He told me to shut up. He pushed me down and took what he came for. Afterwards, he asked me if I came. That says it all really.

We got dressed and headed to the sauna. We might as well have gone to a caravan park. The sauna was about two-hundred-years old (slight exaggeration) and the steam room wasn't hot. For what was meant to be a luxurious evening away, it suddenly became clear that he had found a cheap last-minute deal online and thought it would tempt me back into his arms. I would've rather stayed in than spend ten minutes in a mould-flecked steam room. We both agreed it was a dump and went back to the room and got ready for dinner. I don't know why I am telling you all this. Let's just say that he got what he wanted and had no interest in being in my emotional company. The conversation was lacking in every possible way. He was just going through the motions, having had the shag that he wanted.

That was it. The wake-up call I needed. Obviously, it hadn't always been like that between us, but it definitely had been in the last twelve months. He was tired of my shit and I was tired of his. He dropped me home and I told him it was a mistake before exiting the car. A mistake that would never happen again. He told me that I have to ruin everything and sped off.

The good news, dear diary, is that I haven't had a drink since. I haven't even wanted one. I'm still not going to say never at this point, but I need time to heal. I need to rewire my brain and see my worth. I am not going to have another drink until I love myself. That is my promise to you. I need exercise, I need to eat well, I need to focus at work, and I need to surround myself with good people. I am going to do it. Just you watch me.

Night night, diary.

Big love, Alice xx

February 11th 2019

Dear diary, it's me.

I am loving life! I love the rain watering our plants and the ground. I love beams of sunlight breaking through the clouds and giving us the promise of spring around the corner. I love music. Even the songs I don't like I can appreciate more than I would've done before.

I haven't touched a drop of alcohol for two weeks solid now, making it a total of twenty-nine days this year. I know two weeks isn't long and I'm not sure if I'm imagining it, but my hair seems shinier and thicker. My skin is beginning to look better. It didn't right away, which was disappointing, but I get it. In fact, giving up wasn't great the first week and I can see how many people wouldn't bother. I got a horrendous cold, I had about five mouth ulcers, and then I had a break-out of spots. I don't normally get spots. This wasn't a deterrent for me to quit. This enabled me to continue. It occurred to me that the poison was making its way out. How bad must something be for your body to react in such a bad way? Alcohol really is the juice of the devil. From the minute it passes your lips, you will always need more to feel better due to the damage it causes, or you must go through withdrawal. Every hangover is your body begging you to stop.

I was driving to work the other day and I started to think about all the hangovers I have had. I thought about the times I had been sick, sometimes in my sleep. I thought about the times I had woken up and immedi-ately wanted (and sometimes had) hair of the dog. I thought about the pain, the thumping, the nausea, the sweating, the shame, the anxiety, and realised that every single time my body was pleading with me to stop hurting it. I almost wanted to cry. My body can't phone me up and tell me that it doesn't like the poison I am feeding it. The only thing it can do is to try and reject it, but almost every time it pleaded, I gave it more to take the edge off.

As I was driving along the motorway on autopilot, I began to visualise my body as a separate entity that is being ambushed and beaten to the ground. Every time it tries to get back up, I beat it some more. It begins to cry and tries to tell me it loves me, and it needs me to love it back, and I tell it to shut up and beat it some more.

I then think about all the meaningless sex, the texts that made me look like a bloody idiot, the point-less arguments and drama, the sobbing over a beer table whilst reliving painful events in my life, the bull-shit conversations with women in toilets that I would never see again, the times I risked my job by pulling a sickie or just not being on good form. With two hands on the steering wheel, I shook my head in disbelief that I let all of that happen because I really thought life needed alcohol. Alcohol made me a tart. Alcohol made me a moron. Alcohol made me a bigot. Alcohol made me obnoxious. Alcohol took and took and took. Why couldn't I see that by removing that single toxic habit from my life, I could have a whole new world of possi-bilities?

Don't believe me? You really should. I have woken up from the 'drinking is fun' spell and I now see it for the vampire that it is. Alcohol does nothing for me. It takes. I am a good person and I am doing this to find out what person I was meant to be before I started obliterating what few brain cells I have with alcohol.

In the last two weeks, I have been eating better again, doing some light exercise, and adopting a proper skin care regime. Well, that might be to do with the spot break-out I had, but it's a good habit to have.

The point is: without alcohol I care more. I have started being kinder. I make small talk in shops now, I give people my parking tickets if they have time left on them, I have even started posting little notes to my friends telling them I love them, and that I think they are great.

I do think they are great, and I think it's important they know. I also feel like there is a lack of love and care for me in my life currently, but I realise I may have pushed people away with my selfish and irritable personality that came from excessive drinking. I now believe that I have to be the change that I want to see. If I can't get the love I want, I need to be the love I want.

It all starts with me. I know that now. I know not every day will be sunshine and rainbows, but every single bad thing that happens is manageable and is not made better by self-medicating with alcohol. My stress levels are astronomically reduced by living a pure life. I suppose I feel like there is hope again. When I was drinking, it felt as though there was no hope. There was only addiction. The need for alcohol. The belief that alcohol made every situation better and then the dismay that would come the following morning when you had to admit that you were weak again and that nothing was better for having had those drinks. And now you feel sad too. And anxious. Wow. What a way to start a day.

Each day I wake up, now knowing my body is a little better as I walk along the treacherous path of recovery. Do you know why I'm saying that to you? So that I can address it. It isn't treacherous. I have been reading a lot about quitting and many people talk about the struggle and the cravings. You can't be craving something if your body is free of it. They say that it takes alcohol ten days to leave your body. I would imagine after that, it's psychological. You are romanticising the memory of it. Like an abusive ex-partner. It doesn't need to be torture. For me, it feels like I have been locked in a tower for the last two years. A tiny little tower with a small window to the world outside. Everyday, I would watch people milling about, wishing I could be them. Now, my shackles have been cut, the door has been opened and I am free. The door is still open and if I look inside, there is a bottle of wine open with a glass next to it. On the wall is the shackle. One does not come without the other. No amount of peer pressure, stress, or misery will make me put that shackle back on.

The joy I find in every day menial things is testament to that.

All my love, Alice xx

March 12th 2019

Dear diary, it's me again.

You are probably wondering where I have been. I don't know exactly. Hell and back? Gosh, I had to read the last insert to remind myself of what happened. I don't know what happened. The last chapter was so full of hope. I really sounded convincing, didn't I?

The truth is, it's a whole month later and I can't remember why, but what I can tell you is that there has been a lot of alcohol. I have been shitfaced every night. At least a bottle of wine every night. Sometimes a drink at midday. We had half term. Half term with nowhere to be and all my friends working full-time jobs leaves a very bored Alice.

A bored Alice starts drinking at lunch times, then tries to drink slowly until 5 P.M. to convince herself she is in control, and then cracks open the wine for the evening. At the end of half term was a four-day weekend. That was just one long bender for me. At least it was with friends. For them it was a mini holiday. For me, it was the norm. I can't seem to get a grip on it. Perhaps I was foolish to think that I could do this. I had convinced myself that it was my time. Everyone else laughed at my proclamations and I tutted at their lack of support, but they were right. They might think I am pathetic—hell, I did too this morning when I thought enough was enough, but then I read my last diary insert and I empowered myself. I can get back to that girl.

Two weeks sober sounds like a long shot, so maybe if I have learnt anything, it's that this isn't going to be easy. There may be wobbles; I just can't let that wobble be for two months. That's when you know your drinking is more of an issue than the average Joe. Most people do not get pissed for a whole month solid. As I said at the beginning of this journey, I only have to say no today.

As I say, I can't remember how it started, but I can tell you how I saw all my good work slowly reverse. My diet went out the window, loading up on carbs and crap to soak up the damage. The exercise was reduced to minimal levels because I was so lethargic and lacking in enthusiasm but, overall, the biggest worry was the mental health aspect. The negative thoughts that creep in but increase daily, the withdrawal from society, the crying on your own because you're pissed and sad, the shame in the morning when you wake up on the sofa fully clothed and the lamp still on. It's disgusting. Alcohol is evil and seriously dangerous. I want to find the joy in things again. I want to be friendly and warm. I want people to have a nice experience when they meet me. I want to be so fun or nice or whatever, that people want to spend time with me. These days, it's always me reaching out to friends. Maybe I need new friends. Maybe sober me needs something new.

I can't tell you what happened last night because I can't remember. All I know is that I have woken up hating myself once more and it's time to give this another go. I owe it to me, and I owe it to you, and you never know. If I crack this, then maybe I owe it to anyone I dare lend this diary to at some point in the future. This journey could become a self-help guide, but only if I succeed.

So, let's make some goals.

1. *Don't set unrealistic targets.*
2. *Do not let failure last too long.*
3. *Make notes of successes.*
4. *This is a habit I am breaking, so I will need to make new ones.*
5. *One day at a time. Plan a reward.*

I think that is a good starting point. I have had the wind taken out of my sails. I know I can fail spectacularly, but I could win immeasurably. I can do this. I can do this. I can do this.

Love, Alice xx

March 19th 2019

Dear diary, it's me.

Well, that went well. Not.

It started with one glass and before I knew it, I was back on a bottle a night. By the time I realised I needed to stop, it was three drinks in the afternoon and a bottle and a half a night. It has been a week. One week! How did it spiral so quickly? Is it the talking about it that is making it harder? How can I be so motivated one minute and then not only fail, but drown in losing the next?

Again, let me try and pick my brains here. I was writing to you. Full of confidence and bravado, really believing yet again that I was in control of this fucking monster within me. In fact, I don't think monster is the right word. People see or look at a monster and feel scared. An alcoholic—because let's face it, that's what I fucking am now—looks in the face of alcohol and says 'game on' because there is no fear. There is relief, excitement, a slight dread of the hangover, but that gets elbowed to the back by Mr Party Time. Mr Party Time will not be there in the morning though; by that point, he has been flattened, round-house kicked in the gonads by Mr Hangover. So, if it's not a monster, then what is it? Perhaps it is The Devil. I remember reading something once that said, the Devil would not present itself to you as something to be afraid of. He will come to you with arms open wide to lure you in. That must be it. It is the juice of the Devil and, by God, is he clever.

So, look, I'm back to square one. Difference being … wait … listen … hear me out. The difference being I am writing to you of an evening! I have worked late, even sent the boss an email at 8 P.M. which probably threw him a bit. I have done some cleaning, I cooked a homemade meal and put the leftovers in containers and into the freezer. None of that stuff gets done when the wine comes out. It's like if I don't drink, I achieve so much, but one glass of wine and that's it for the evening. I know I have told you that before, but not only am I trying to get the message into my thick, bloody brain, I am hoping this might help someone else one day. I have had my daily quota of water and I am alcohol-free. This has got to be the first time in a few weeks.

I need to get to the root of the trigger or triggers, but at the same time I don't want to give it too much thought. I'm worried that talking about it only conjures up cravings.

I am also aware, at this point, that if I don't change the broken sodding record soon, this diary of mine won't help anyone.

Ok, let's have a roundup of the positives that have come out of today; I had a lie-in, which wasn't exactly planned, but because I didn't get smashed last night, meant I wasn't awake at 5 A.M. with a mouth like a lost property flip-flop. I woke up with more energy and in a pretty good mood because I wasn't hungover. I did drink yesterday, but not as much as normal, and had plenty of water before I went to bed. I guess that has triggered today.

The sheer positivity that came from me with no difference to my life other than yesterday ... that alcohol intake is always a good motivator. So, had a good sleep and have been in a great mood. I wasn't a bitch to anyone at work and I was polite and focused all day.

When I got home, instead of opening the fridge for my 'reward', I got changed and went for a brisk walk in the sun and that was a far better reward. Don't get me wrong, when 5 P.M. hit, I couldn't stop thinking about alcohol and I drove all the way home arguing with myself not to stop at the shop. As soon as I got in, I got changed and went straight back out. It was one hundred percent the right decision.

I urge you to get past the 5 P.M. wanker that says you deserve a drink. 6 P.M. loves you when it wins against 5 P.M. The rest of the evening is a doddle. Like I said, I decided to log on and do some work emails, not saying you have to, but I had the foresight to check my diary and tomorrow is a busy one, so I sent out some emails early to get ahead of the game. Then I sat down to watch some television and found that this little diary of mine here was niggling away. I was thinking I was too tired for it tonight. Tired? Lazy more like. I want to write a diary that either helps me get a grip, helps someone else, or both. It occurred to me that whoever wrote the TV programme I was watching did not get there by sitting around watching other people's stuff. The only way to be successful is to just do whatever it is that you want to do. Just do it. No ifs, no buts. Do. It. Like the old Chinese proverb quotes, never underestimate small actions. Even tiny raindrops will eventually fill a vessel. Just do it.

The final part of today's success story is that I can now go to bed and read. Reading is good for the mind; it's good for vocabulary and grammar, and it's a good sleep aid. It's none of those things when you have sunk a bottle of sparkling white.

So, on that lovely cheery note, I shall bid thee

farewell as I begin my ablutions and prepare for a restful night ahead.

Oh yeah, one more thing. It's Monday. I achieved all that on a Monday. Mondays are just as appealing as Fridays when you have a lot to be happy about. Who knew?!

Night night.

Love, Alice xx

April 12th

Dear diary, it's me.

By now, you know that I am either here to confess or preach. I think today's diary entry is going to be a bit of both. I have been drinking, but I am ok. I keep trying to rationalise every fucked-up thought I have and have concluded that maybe I am not an alcoholic. Maybe I am just fucked-up and alcohol is my cure.

Hear me out. I seem to do everything to extremes. Not normal. Alcohol subdues me. I just need to control this coping mechanism so that it doesn't end up controlling me. Let's look at the facts. I drink and on day one it is fun. Day two, it is about recovery and taking the edge off how shit I feel. By day three, it is inevitably closer to the weekend, so why stop now? Classic fucked-up thought processes. Now, the flip side is that I do one day sober and think I am Gandhi. The high lasts for twenty-four hours and like a classic fucked-up thinker, I am not satiated. I am looking for my next thrill.

Sober doesn't work because I have just done that. I've made my point, so why not have another drink, and alternate your days, and have a day on followed by a day off, and so on? When I don't drink, I cannot sleep. That can't be right? I read somewhere once that in the olden days they gave psychiatric patients alcohol to make them sleep. So, there you have it. I'm a psycho. Give the psycho alcohol and all that will happen is that she will become depressed. So? Deprive the psycho and who knows what will become of her? Yikes.

I also think I am an over-thinker. I know you are laughing now. Lol. Seriously, I beat myself up about everything. Am I a psycho? Unlikely. Am I an alcoholic? Very likely. Who am I kidding? I just need to keep writing it all out, find some kind of pattern, or do something disgraceful and have that wake-up call that self-confessed alcoholics have so that I get a grip once and for all? I am weak, and I am pathetic. I know that much. I'm going to go and pour myself a drink now. I know that you are screaming at me not to, but why not? There is nothing else to do and I can hear what you are saying, but I am actually not better than that. This is me. What is the worst that could happen?

Night night, Alice xx

April 28th 2019

Dear diary,

I am so sick of my own shit. I am sick of the bull-shit that spews out of my mouth. I am sick of being jealous of those who are living the good life. I am sick of people with confidence. I am sick of kind people. I am sick of my weakness. I am sick of the noise inside my head. I don't want to drink anymore.

I DO NOT WANT TO DRINK ANYMORE.

It is ruining my life. It can never be one drink when it comes to me. It has to be a whole bottle of wine and that third and fourth glass make me sad and ruins tomorrow. It ruins my sleep. It ruins my self-esteem and it invites tomorrow's boozy session in.

Why can't I do this? Why am I so pathetic? I have read a couple of the quit lit books out there and you know what? Yeah, at first, they worked. I felt like I was on cloud nine for about a week, but then I would tell myself I am overreacting, that I am not an alcoholic, and it would be ok to have a little binge. Except that binge never would be little. In fact, they have been getting longer. I am drinking more now than when I sodding started this self-help diary. Between you and me, I'm pretty sure I took cocaine last night. I can't really remember. Yesterday was one long, mad blowout.

I had decided that it was time, and to put this gremlin to bed, I was going to go out with a bang. When I woke up earlier this morning, everything was a blur. I trudged downstairs to get a glass of water and went back to bed. This afternoon, when I finally peeled my pathetic arse out of bed, I still struggled to make any sense of the night before. Something didn't seem right, but my brain was too mashed up to piece anything together. I was half un-dressed and nothing seemed to make any sense really. I had really overdone it this time. A wave of panic washed over me as I thought about the drugs. I was definitely offered it. I remember that, but I don't know what happened next. I don't know how I got home, how I have a cut on my head and a sore wrist. I was just grateful that I woke up alone and could feel sorry in my pit with no one to explain myself to.

I want to be free. I know now that my relationship with alcohol has changed forever. What started out as fun has become tainted and no matter how many days or weeks I managed to abstain, it is never fun to go back. Almost immediately after the first sip, I get louder, more opinionated, more obnoxious. Trouble begins to rise to the surface, and it might not be visible to everyone else, but it's trouble every time alright. It's the green-eyed monster feeling envious of the pretty girl having fun. It's the 'insecurity witch' telling me how worthless I am and that I need to drink up to drown out her criticisms. It's the damaged girl picking a fight with her boyfriend over nothing apart from a self-sabotage of believing it will never work out, so I had better get in there first and end it. I don't have fun like the majority of you.

Are you having fun, or are we all lying to ourselves? I can't remember the last time it was fun. All I know is that I have been doing it out of addiction and I don't know for how long.

I am not going to sit here and promise you that I have got a grip on it. I have tried that a few times now and failed spectacularly. I am going to tell you that I am going to try. I do not want to drink. It does not do any good for me. The penny has finally dropped. I haven't felt this determined in months. It's the first time, however, that I am not bouncing off the walls with false hope. I actually feel really moody. I think sober me is sick of my shit too. I have to prove it to me this time. I can rid myself of alcohol and become the woman that God intended me to be.

One thing I have always quite enjoyed is being smug. Not in a 'I'm better than you' way, just in the celebratory way. Who doesn't love to celebrate (there lies the problem)? You don't have to be an asshole because you are good at something. The British culture seems to have a problem with celebrating other people's successes, but they sure as hell love celebrating for no reason. Anyway, I want to be sober and smug. If you have ever taken a sip of alcohol after some time off, have you noticed how disgusting it actually tastes? We don't need it. Or I don't need it. It doesn't make things better. It makes everything worse and I mean everything. It dulls the sparkle in a celebration. It makes heartache unbearable.

God, if you are listening. I need your help. Release me from this evil. Free me of this poison so that I may become a better person and actually contribute some good to this earth whilst I live on it.

Love, Alice.

April 29ᵗʰ 2019

Dear diary,

Well, you're not my diary. You're a scrap piece of paper. You're not my diary and this is barely my writing. My hands are shaking, and I feel weak.

I am in big trouble. I have been arrested and I am in prison. I am being charged for a hit-and-run. I am so scared. I don't remember anything.

How could I let something like this happen? I am so ashamed. I hate myself. This is my biggest nightmare and I can't remember anything about it. All I know is that I got very drunk the night before and it was my car, so it must've been me. I must've got blackout drunk and now I might've killed someone.

I wish it was me that I had killed.

Alice.

1

HANNAH

'Rosie. Rosie. Good girl. Come on.' Hannah patted both her hands on her squatted knees and watched the beautiful brown Labrador come bounding over to her, her back legs nearly in front of her body, leading the way as she galloped towards her.

Rosie's chestnut eyes were like saucers and leaking with love. She jumped up on her owner, unaware of her own stature almost taking Hannah down.

Hannah ruffled her ears and made cooing noises over the dog she adored. She talked to Rosie as if she were her baby. The baby she longed for that had never arrived. She and Craig had spent the last two years trying, but nothing. Hannah had actually tried for the last three years, unbeknownst to her husband. She had suggested IVF, but Craig kept avoiding it. He said they just needed to keep trying and to relax.

Craig was an overachiever. He had excelled in every area of his life. Hannah knew he was not going to let a doctor tell him he had weak sperm, if that was what it was. She wasn't going to give up on her dream.

For now, she would keep praying for a miracle and showing Craig what a good mother she was to Rosie.

Hannah held out her hand to Rosie, who licked the cooked chicken in one big wet swoop and swallowed it down before immediately pleading for more with her stare and a slight head tilt. She rubbed her between the ears and looked longingly into her big brown eyes. Sighing at the love she had to give and the baby she wanted to receive it.

Hannah and Rosie had been for a long walk through the woods behind their house. Craig was out playing tennis with one of his friends, so Hannah poured herself a glass of wine and went and sat in the conservatory with a book, *Chill Out and Conceive The Easy Way*. She placed it on her lap and had a sip of her wine before putting it on the floor next to her feet.

They had everything apart from a baby. Craig had his own software company that he had set up in his bedroom after university. He now had over five-hundred staff in several offices up and down the country. Hannah was a speech therapist. They both loved what they did and had a very nice life because of it. Craig was respected within his field and was often invited to be a keynote speaker at tech events, and Hannah was established enough to set up her own clinic, which was thriving and distinguished. They enjoyed three holidays a year. They drove around in the luxurious cars they'd both wanted and had all the gadgets a person could need. They could do clothes shopping without checking the price tags. Their house was elegant with expensive pieces of artwork and the odd sculpture strategically placed here and there. Marble floors. Chandeliers. They had what most people dreamed of ... apart from the family they craved.

Craig was out most weekends, playing sports with his friends. This was becoming more frequent and Hannah knew it was the baby talk that was driving a wedge between them. She was getting lonely and becoming worried that they were drifting apart when baby-making very much needed them to be together.

Most of her friends had children now and she felt ostracised. She felt like they spoke a different language because of it, and she didn't fit in. Every time there was a girl's night it would be all baby talk and she couldn't relate. If she tried to chip in, they would laugh at her, and tell her to wait. They told her she had no idea. She knew she had had no idea, but they had no idea of how sad that made her.

She picked up the book again and took another sip of wine. Before she knew it, she had gotten to the bottom of the page she was on and realised she hadn't taken in a single word of it. Placing the book down again, she stood up and took a big gulp of her wine. Staring out of the conservatory windows, looking into space. She imagined one of those little slides in the corner near the pond. That would have to go when the time came. 'Ponds and babies don't mix,' she thought. She would get Craig to make a rope swing for the child's fourth birthday. She would be out there tidying up the flowerbeds and their little person would be helping with their own plastic garden set. She would like a boy first and then a girl. Her son would be blonde and blue-eyed and her daughter would have flame-coloured ringlets. She had a list of names for each on her phone, which she added to and removed some regularly.

She finished her wine and walked gloomily back to the kitchen. Reading was hopeless. She was not in the mood. She wished Craig would just spend a lazy afternoon with her at home. Maybe they could conceive if they had impromptu sex one day rather than it always being at bedtime. Recently, it seemed as if he wasn't even enjoying it. It seemed too planned. Hannah knew he was fed up, but she knew a baby would change everything. She just needed to get pregnant soon.

Hannah slumped down into their corner sofa and pulled a cushion to her chest. She flicked on the television and found a chick flick that she had seen many times before but made for perfect Sunday viewing. She knew she wouldn't be able to concentrate on a new film so this was ideal. Her phone lit up and her heart sank as it was another message from Craig telling her he was going for a beer with Danny and wouldn't be back until later. She would have to speak to him about this. Just because she had been talking about babies a lot did not mean he could try to pretend she or the problem didn't exist. She thought she could say to him that if he could just get her pregnant, then he could be out as much as he wanted, as she would be busy as a new mum anyway. She pondered that thought and was disappointed and excited simultaneously that that idea might actually work for him.

She logged on to Facebook and started scrolling. So many of her friends were enjoying a family Sunday. Cooking a big lunch for one another, uploading funny photos of their toddlers and the chaos that was happening around them. Grandparents giving some of them some time off as they were hungover or on a spa day. The more she scrolled, the more annoyed she got that everyone had the life she wanted. Did she have kids? No. Was she hungover? Also no. Were they having a romantic day together? No, siree. Did she want a spa day? Yep.

Craig would rather spend the morning out running, followed by an afternoon of tennis with Danny and then a beer with Danny. When he returned, he would have a shower, put on his lounge clothes, and sit on his laptop doing emails in preparation for his week ahead. She could make them dinner and he would appreciate it, but he would appreciate a takeaway just as much. She wasn't going to cook for him today. This had been going on for a couple of months now. She didn't mind at first, but she was not going to spend the afternoon in the kitchen alone, just for him to wolf it down and hand her his plate to take away. She desperately wanted to be a mother, but not to her husband.

As she scrolled through her phone, browsing the internet, she noticed adverts for pregnancy vitamins and classes and such. It got her thinking that there must be groups on there for people who couldn't or didn't yet have children. She did a quick search and was amazed by how many forums there were. She went down the list and requested to join several of them. One of them accepted her immediately. Suddenly, she didn't feel bored or lonely and was glad that Craig was out. Excited, she leapt up from the sofa and poured herself another glass of wine and then returned to her spot and pulled a blanket over her. Sitting comfortably, she started looking through the page and took great comfort in what she was reading. Many women had taken a long time to conceive. Some needed additional help, some just needed time.

There were lots of success stories, but there was also a fair bit of heartache. She decided to write her own post and introduce herself.

'Hi Everyone, I have just joined. I have been feeling so low for so long. My husband and I are desperate for a baby, and it just isn't happening. We haven't sought help; he doesn't want to. He is fit and so am I. We don't drink much and neither of us smoke. I know we just have to be patient. Logging in here today has provided me with much comfort and hope. I just wanted to say hi. Hope you're all having a good weekend. Han x'

Within seconds she started getting likes on the post and within minutes she was getting comments. She smiled as she read them and thought this might be the perfect place for her over the coming weeks.

2

PHIL

'Come on, you beauty!' Phil roared at the television mounted above his line of vision as fragments of peanuts spluttered from his mouth. He waved his betting slip as if it would make the horse go faster. It didn't, so he screwed it up in his fist and brought it down to the countertop in a rage. 'Fuck!'

More peanut shrapnel escaped his mouth, some remaining in the corners of his mouth and some landing on his chin. Perched with his legs wide open and a stomach that had endured years of poor diet and excess alcohol spilling over his waistband. His once white polo shirt was not the only thing that had seen better days.

Disgruntled and beaten, he slid off the stool and left the betting shop. Some kids were playing with a football in the car park and it crossed his path. He knelt to retrieve the ball that had tapped against his bust-up trainers and brought it to his chest.

'Oi slim, give us our ball back.'

The young men sniggered.

'That's no way to talk to me; ask for it nicely,' Phil said with an almost buried air of superiority.

'Give us our ball back ... sir.'

Phil smirked and rolled the ball back towards them.

'Fat prick,' one of them muttered under their breath.

Before Phil could see which one it was, they had turned and were running away, laughing indiscreetly. Phil grimaced and made the short walk back towards his pub. He passed a young mother on the way there. Mouth gaping, he eyeballed her up and down.

'Get real,' she said with a disgusted look on her face.

Phil laughed at himself. The youngsters were getting ruder by the day. He thought back to when he was a PE teacher in the local secondary school. They would never have gotten away with it then. The adults didn't take that kind of crap back then. Back then, everyone knew their place. Everyone knew where they were in the pecking order—everyone apart from Lyndsey Palmer. He clenched his teeth at his own annoyance for allowing her to creep back into his head. That little tart continued to haunt him, even after all these years.

He unlocked the pub doors and knelt to pick up his post, farting as he did so, arse crack on view for anyone passing.

Steve from the kitchen was already in.

'Alright, Steve. You're early today. Missus kicked you out?' He laughed at what he thought was a funny joke, which quickly developed into a hoarse coughing fit from the years of primary and secondary smoking.

'I'm cleaning the lines, Phil. People have been complaining about the beer for weeks and you don't seem to take any notice.'

'Well, that's very good of you, Steve. Thanks.'

'If this place gets shut down, I'm out of a job. I'm not doing it for you.'

Phil tutted and did an overt eye roll. He reached over the bar, putting further pressure on his polo shirt, and yanked off a packet of pork scratchings form the hanger before settling on a stool and turning on the television.

Steve watched him make himself comfortable and shook his head.

'What?' Phil asked without taking his eyes away from the darts he had put on.

'Shall I get you a drink, Phil?'

'Thought you'd never ask.'

Phil had bought the Red Lion from an inheritance payment his late aunt had left him. She was the wealthy sister of his mother and had never had any children of her own. She had a successful cleaning business and employed over two-hundred cleaners. She had the cleaning contracts in all the business parks in town and she had the cleaning contract at the secondary school where Phil worked, until he was dismissed. Her pride in her work and her reputation had secured those contracts for over twenty years. When he was sacked after Lyndsey Palmer's accusations, she couldn't face the shame he had brought upon the family and so she sacrificed the school contract.

She was slight in frame, so no one really noticed how thin she had become before it was too late. She was a workaholic and had always been skinny. It was only when she started to look gaunt that people urged her to see a doctor. She had known for months that something was up but being the control freak and perfectionist that she was, she couldn't bear hearing that something was wrong with her; that was out of her control.

The blood she passed when she went to the loo told her everything she needed to know. The pain that began to increase in her abdomen and the drastic weight loss. She knew it was advanced and she knew it was a battle she could not face. She didn't want the hair loss. She didn't want the colostomy bag. She didn't want the intrusion and the constant mithering. She decided to ignore it and get everything put into place for when it was time. She set up a will and left a hefty amount to Phil, her only nephew. Her sister, Phil's mother, couldn't make any sense of it. Until she got her own with the note, that was. She hadn't wanted him to be a burden on her and so she had given him the money only to leave her sister, his mother, alone. Helen knew that he would struggle to work after the Lyndsey Palmer scandal. She couldn't take the shame away for her sister, but she could take away the burden.

3

———

OLLIE

Ollie pulled the scooped neck of his t-shirt down and away from him and sprayed an unnecessary amount of Old Spice onto his young chest. He looked in the mirror. His hair was coated in lashings of wet-look gel, which he hoped would detract from the unwelcome pimples and whiteheads that tormented him. His branded t-shirt he had found in a charity shop for a couple of quid. He loved shopping in charity shops but would take the train to the next town so that he wouldn't bump into any of the pricks from school. They made his life hard enough as it was, let alone catching him buying second-hand goods.

Nothing he did was good enough for the school bullies. They slagged off his cheap trainers and when he managed to find a pair of cool ones in a charity shop, they suggested he'd nicked them. When he found that really cool jacket and wore it in, thinking they might like him a bit more now that he had the same clothes as them, they laughed and said his mum had probably shagged someone to get it for him. When he got his ear pierced, they said he looked like a bender. When he retorted that he wasn't, he got slammed against the locker whilst one of them tugged on it, making it bleed, and told him not to answer back.

Ollie didn't have a bad bone in his body. He was desperate to fit in. He tried everything, but everything he could think of only seemed to make things worse. If anyone tried to be friends with him, then they would get bullied too, so they never hung around for long. He became a loner and although he hated it, it was the safest way to be. He had plans of moving abroad and becoming someone new when he was older. Someone successful. Someone cool. The type of guy that people would go up to him and say hello as he entered the room, not turn their back on him and shuffle awkwardly away.

It began as far back as he could remember. His father had never been in the picture. He had early memories of a birthday card and a toy a couple of times, but he must've been about five. His father certainly hadn't sent anything for about ten years now. His mother had said it was good, but he wished he could've been allowed to make that decision for himself. He would rather have known that his father wasn't worth having around instead of being told. For most of his childhood he had believed her, but now that he was becoming a young man, he had questions of his own. There was stuff he wanted to know. Did he have his father's temper? Did he have his father's insecurities, or was he insecure because of his father? Was his father cool? Did he get unwanted sandwiches thrown at him on the walk home from school? Or had he ever been that kid? That thought made him feel uneasy. It occurred to him that karma might not just affect you. It might affect the ones you love. Maybe his father had been the bully and karma was hurting Ollie. Ollie thought that if people thought more like that, then perhaps we wouldn't have any bullies.

Satisfied with his odour and hair gel, he shrugged in the mirror, knowing it would make no difference to his day. He would either be ignored, or he would be tormented. He wouldn't be welcomed. He wouldn't be offered a seat in the canteen. No one would say hi as he entered the school gates. It would be another day of loneliness and trying to blend in, no doubt.

He picked up his beaten-up old school bag and slung it over his shoulder. 'Bye Mum!' he called out and didn't get a response. It was no surprise to him. He quietly turned the latch on the door and pulled it closed discreetly. He wasn't sure what time she had come in last night, but it was late, he knew that much.

He thought how nice it would be to listen to some music on his walk into school, but last time he did that he hadn't heard Ewan Scott come running up behind him and slam him into a tree. He had been winded instantly and the pain surged through his body. His iPod skimmed across the pavement in front of them and as he put out his hand to grab it, a heavy foot came down on his and he heard several cracks. The scream he let out suggested two broken fingers. The rest of the boys laughed and called him a wimp.

Ewan picked up the iPod and began howling. 'He's listening to Eric Clapton. What a loser.'

The boys all laughed and jeered. Ollie wanted to tell them that Eric Clapton was better than anyone they listened to, but he knew better, and he was sure Eric would tell him to keep his mouth shut in this situation as well. Ewan tossed the iPod into the road like a used cigarette and Ollie watched in slow motion as a waste-bin lorry came hurtling towards it and crushed it in one quick tyre swoop. The bullies walked off, leaving Ollie whimpering on the ground with questions of why spinning around his head.

Ever since that day, he had decided to remove that risk and not listen to music again whilst walking. He concluded it would be much safer and wiser to keep his wits about him.

As he entered the school gates, a girl pushed passed him but immediately apologised. Ollie looked to his side in disbelief. She was new. Now it made sense. She had black afro hair with flashes of purple through it. It was tied up in a messy ponytail but looked very cool. She had stud earrings going up her earlobes until the space ran out. Her eyes were outlined with winged eyeliner. She had a nose ring. Ollie was mesmerised. She wore a purple hoodie that matched the streaks in her hair and had a short skirt teamed with fishnets and Doc Martins.

She looked at Ollie looking at her. 'What?' She blew a big bubblegum bubble and it burst across her full lips. She used her tongue to pull it back into her mouth.

Ollie was transfixed. 'Sorry. It's just that ... no one has ever said sorry to me before.'

She looked confused and carried on her way into the school, and he watched her take a seat in reception. She must be a similar age to him he thought, despite looking older. All the girls in his year looked older than they were and certainly older than the boys of their age.

Ollie trundled along, wondering how long it would be before she hated him too.

The bell sounded and the bustling corridor quietened as the pupils dissipated into their various class-rooms, like ants disappearing into the ground. As Ollie entered his tutor room, it occurred to him how most teenagers would love to have the superpower of invisibility, and yet he was living and breathing it. No one noticed him enter the room, no one noticed him pull out a chair and put his bag on his desk and sit down alone. No one cared. No one in his class would notice if he was there or not.

Mrs Paterson called the class to attention and offered Ollie a pensive smile. She worried about him. She thought about him more than any of her other students. She knew he faced a hard time everyday at school and she knew his mother was an alcoholic. She didn't think his mother was a bad person, but she did think she was very lost and as a result, her son was lost at an earlier age than she was, and that concerned Mrs Paterson. She knew Ollie would grow up either breaking the mould or becoming a statistic. There was no in-between for boys like him and it made her heart heavy. She couldn't intervene. The one time she tried to talk to him, one of the bullies overhead and made it worse for him. They both knew they could talk in private and they both knew they never would. Ollie never put his hand up in class, he entered the room last, and left the room last.

Just as Mrs Paterson had finished the register, there was a knock at the door and in came the new girl. Ollie felt a warmth come over his body. His shoulders relaxed and he felt at ease as she looked and him and offered a smile.

'Everyone, this is Sky. I am sure you will all make her feel very welcome. Please take a seat Sky and we all hope you have a great first day with us. I'm sure you will settle in nicely.'

The classroom of students soaked up Sky's outfit and wild hair whilst she skimmed the room for an empty seat, completely nonchalant to the gazes of wonderment she was getting. She walked right up to Ollie and pulled out the chair next to him. He jumped as she dropped her bag onto the desk they were now sharing. If any of the bullies were making any noises, his heart beating in his ears was drowning it out.

He was almost too scared to look at her, but the desire to look into her eyes was fierce. He tried, and failed, to take a subtle look and was dazzled further by her beaming white smile.

'Hi,' she mouthed whilst chewing on her gum. She looked at him, giving him her full attention and he didn't know how to handle it.

'Hi,' Ollie murmured, quieter than a mouse.

The bell rang, signalling the end of the lesson. Ollie stood up and packed his bag and prepared to make his way to the next class alone. The 'back-row boys', as he called them, because they sat in the back row of every lesson heckling students and teachers and causing a general disruption, were making eyes at Sky.

'Shame you had to sit next to that loser,' one of them piped up. 'You should come and sit with us in the next class. Ollie is the class freak. Everyone knows that. Best to find out early before he tries to take you under his manky little wing.'

Ollie could feel his stomach frown. He was afraid he would never get to have a friend of his own.

'I can make my own decisions, thank you', said

Sky as she continued to pack her bag without even looking at them.

'Of course you can, gorgeous, but I'm just giving you the heads up that that one there is a wrong 'un'. A right little weirdo,' her admirer kept on.

Sky zipped up her bag and walked up to the boy so that their noses were almost touching.

'Listen here, you little arse goblin. The only issue I can see right now is you being a horrible little prick. I never have and never will make an assumption on the opinion of others, least of all some little cock weasel like you, and whilst we are at it, if you speak about him like that again in front of me, you'll be tasting tarmac. Understood?'

Sky linked arms with Ollie and frog-marched him out of the classroom, leaving the back-row boys with their jaws almost on the floor.

Mrs Paterson smirked as she heard one the boys repeat 'arse goblin'. She hoped Ollie and Sky would become great friends.

4

HANNAH

A week had passed, and Hannah and Craig had only slept together once. There had been no romance leading up to it. No passionate tussle in bed. No words and no foreplay. He had actually gotten out of bed and was heading for the en suite when Hannah stroked his muscular thigh with her toes. He hesitated and got back into bed, not because he wanted it, but because he didn't want a hard time. He climbed on top and dodged her attempt at kissing him and buried his face into her shoulder. He was barely in the mood for sex, let alone her morning breath.

Fed up and exhausted from being a performing monkey, he let his mind drift off as he tried to muster up the desire to have sex with his wife. He hadn't wanted to have sex with Hannah since she had started making sex a diary entry activity. He found himself thinking of Hayley at the tennis club. She was far too young for him, but she smiled so sweetly at him whenever he saw her. They had barely spoken and yet he often found himself hoping she was working each time he went there. He remembered the image of her playing in the courts next to him one day. As he walked past to go into his regular pre-booked court, she was bending over to pick up the ball and he caught a glimpse of her bronzed peachy derrière escaping out of her tiny white shorts—and just like that, he came. He pulled out of Hannah quickly.

'No wait, Craig! You are meant to leave it in for a few minutes,' shrieked Hannah.

'Fuck sake, Hannah.' He leapt out of bed and headed for the en suite. 'This is *not* turning me on.' He slammed the door behind him.

Hannah gulped back the lump that was making itself known in her throat. 'Fuck you,' she whispered under her breath before throwing off the covers. She stormed into the bathroom and got in the shower with him, almost pushing him aside in a rage.

'What are you doing?' barked Craig, sounding even more annoyed.

Hannah grabbed the shower head and put it between her legs, rinsing away anything that was left, and douching what was inside.

'Hannah, baby, what are you doing?' Craig saw the sadness in her eyes and suddenly felt his stomach knot. He could give her everything. All the clothes. All the jewellery. Anything. Anything but the baby she so desperately wanted.

'Fuck you, Craig.' She exited the cubicle, grabbed her dressing gown, and slammed the door harder than he had.

She stormed down the stairs, the blood pumping quickly around her head and got a teaspoon out of the drawer, almost bending it in half. Her hand shook as she put the spoon in the coffee jar, spilling some on the solid oak worktop as she put it in the cup. She flicked on the kettle and felt steam coming out of her ears as quickly as it came out of the spout.

As the kettle clicked and began to rest, she exhaled and found herself relaxing. She shook her head from side to side, leaning against the counter when suddenly she felt two hands on her hips. Then she felt his soft lips on her neck as he planted tiny, gentle kisses on her.

'I'm sorry,' he whispered.

She tilted her head back and he sucked her neck teasingly. She moaned. He pulled her dressing gown to the side and teased her with his hard on. She opened her legs and he thrust into her. She gasped. He thrust again. She pushed back. He grabbed her hair and wrapped it around his knuckles. She moaned harder. He grabbed her breasts, kissing her heavier on the neck now, and she groaned loudly as she got much wetter. He thrust and thrust again until he came and kept her bent over the worktop.

'Stay,' he whispered. 'Keep me in you.'

She smiled to herself as goosebumps ran across her body. 'Twice in one morning. You can keep that coming.' She pulled him around her and they enjoyed each other silently for a moment longer.

The next two weeks passed by blissfully. Hannah and Craig began enjoying each other's company again. She had relaxed and so had he. He had come home earlier than expected most evenings. Sometimes he would cook and a couple of times they had had early evening sex. He told her they needed to make the most of their alone time before their lives changed forever. He said he felt like they would be pregnant any day now and she said she felt like she already could be.

She didn't want to get their hopes up, but she felt different this time. She felt warm all the time, she had a feeling of contentment residing within her. Something had changed and all she could think was that she must be pregnant this time. When Craig was around, they couldn't keep their hands off each other and when Hannah was alone, she spent most of her time online looking at baby clothes and chatting to her virtual friends in the 'Trying To Get Pregnant' forum. She had posted in there about how excited she was, how she felt different, and this time she really believed something had happened. Her post received numerous comments from her new mum friends, saying when it happened for them, they also 'just knew'. Hannah was overcome with excitement.

Almost two weeks after the kitchen sideboard sex, Hannah was desperate to do a test. Her breasts were sore, she had been getting headaches and feeling nauseous. She was tingling with suspense. She decided to make one more romantic dinner for her and Craig before committing to nine months of sobriety beginning tomorrow, when she would do a test in the morning.

As her Italian chicken simmered on the hob, Hannah looked at the table she had laid immaculately. A single candelabra in the middle, two place settings positioned symmetrically, cutlery glistening in the moody lighting. She smiled at what a perfect wife she was and then skipped up the stairs to find the sexiest outfit she had.

Looking at her walk-in wardrobe, she thought back to when they had bought this house and how thrilled she was at having her own walk-in wardrobe. She'd told all her friends, she'd sent them all pictures; they had all been round and each admired it with a glass of wine, as if it was the opening of a designer store. She sighed as she thought about how much things had changed. None of her friends could care less about her walk-in wardrobe now ... and now, she was the one jealous of what they had. They all had their little families and she felt like the odd one out—and cut off.

Putting her hand on her stomach, she whispered, 'If you are in there, I will love you and care for you so much, I promise.'

She smiled, took a sip of her wine, feeling immediately guilty in case she was in the family way but so nervous that she felt she needed it. As she ran her fingers along one of the dress rails, she found the little black velvet number that she had worn when Craig won the 'Entrepreneur of the Year' award. It was figure-hugging and fell off the shoulders and down into a V-shape around the cleavage. Classic, vintage, sexy. Perfect for tonight. For the last night, just the two of them.

Craig came in the front door downstairs just as she was finishing applying her lipstick. She had gone for classic chic. Her blonde hair had a wave in it, her make-up sultry but not heavy. She made her way to the top of the stairs and paused at the top. Craig had picked up the post on the side and was sifting through it.

'Ahem.' Hannah cleared her throat.

Craig looked up. 'Wow!' He looked her up and down, taking her all in. 'Honey, you look incredible.'

Hannah glided down this stairs and Craig put his hands on her hips and began kissing her neck.

'Na-ah-ah. Dinner first.'
'Can I have *you* for dinner?'
'I'm dessert.'
He grabbed her hand and put it on his hard groin. She smiled and gave it a gentle squeeze.

5

—

PHIL

Phil was in his flat that he lived in above his pub. It was midday and the curtains were still drawn. A haze of cigarette smoke hung just beneath the ceiling. The carpet was scattered with crisp wrappers, beer cans strewn across the floor and other rubbish he was too lazy to take on the short walk to the kitchen bin. There was a selection of pornographic magazines by the end of the sofa with a discarded sock on top.

Thick dust covered the surfaces. Drink stains on the carpet, old and new. Walls that once were a clean magnolia, now looked dirty with various marks all over the place. The place looked as though it hadn't been cleaned in years. The odd broken curtain hooks across the rail left the curtains draping messily. Dirty clothes scattered across the floor. Old newspapers piled up. Not even a picture hung straight on the wall.

Phil was in his bedroom, if you could call it that. It just about accommodated his double bed with a chest of drawers at the end. Each side of the bed had piles of clothes and useless clutter. There was no room to swing a cat, as they said.

He was hunched over his laptop with his hand in his pants. He was looking at Alice's facebook profile. She had been in the pub a few times with friends and he fancied her. Her account was public and as he scrolled through her photos of her trip to Mykonos last summer, he started tugging on his cock. It didn't bother him that her boyfriend was in the pictures. He zoomed in on her crotch in a bikini shot and began to tug harder. The next photo she was walking out of the swimming pool, dripping wet and laughing. That was enough to get him there. He came in his pants and rubbed it all over his penis and balls. He rubbed the remaining off on his pants and closed his laptop shut.

Feeling lighter on his feet, he smiled to himself as he sauntered into the kitchen. There was no worktop in sight as it was so cluttered with discarded half-eaten pot noodles, sandwiches, and microwaveable meals. He retrieved a pasty from the fridge, opened it, and began eating it as if he hadn't eaten for a while, not caring that he hadn't washed his hands.

He looked at the clock and scarfed down the remainder of his pasty and headed for the door.

One of his barmaids was mopping the floors as he made his grand entrance. He stopped and stared at her bending over. Feeling as though she was being watched, she immediately stood up and stared back at him with a look of disgust. Phil asked if he could squeeze past to get behind the bar whilst casually scratching his backside. He picked up the sky remote, got himself a packet of crisps, and perched himself at the end of the bar in his usual spot.

Steve arrived and greeted his boss in an obligatory fashion. Phil asked him to pour him a beer and Steve obliged. He put it down on the bar for him and made his way into the kitchen.

The barmaid, Stacey, followed him in.

'I can't bear being on my own with him in here. He creeps me out.'

Steve put on his white chef's coat and washed his hands. 'Don't worry about Phil. He's a perv, sure, but he would never act on it.'

Stacey looked askance, back at Steve.

'And if he did, he will have me to answer to.'

Stacey looked down and smiled sheepishly. She loved Steve and could see herself very easily falling in love with him. She had been watching him from afar for the last six months, since she started cleaning the pub. She was a young single mother whose self-esteem had been obliterated by her ex. She'd been timid and nervous when she started working. She hadn't taken the job for the money—well, the fact that it was cash in hand was a big incentive. She couldn't afford to work and pay child care. Her mum had told her to get a little part-time job and she would have Isaac. She could commit to that but nothing more. Her mother had hated the way she had been left by her ex and was desperate to see her once vibrant daughter thrive again. Little Isaac was too much for her over a long period, but she could handle a couple of shifts a week to help get Stacey back on her feet. Stacey agreed and as the months passed she started feeling lighter. She thought back to her first shift, when she cleaned the pub from top to bottom just to avoid making conversation or eye contact with anyone. The past had taught her that even a wrong look could cause a smack round the face.

Steve had changed everything for her. He didn't

take no for an answer, not like that, but he kept prob-ing, making jokes, and asked questions that weren't the standard boring chitchat. She didn't want to tell him anything at first, and a few times she thought she had offended him and felt guilty as he had looked crestfallen when she didn't take him on. That made her feel useless as well.

As the weeks passed, she found herself being drawn to Steve's kitchen and wanting to talk to him and ask *him* the questions. Before long, the desire crept in, and she found herself watching for him coming through the pub door. Then the butterflies came and then she found herself enjoying music again, and that's when she knew there was no way out. That had been going on for about three months now. She would always go into the kitchen once she had finished cleaning, and she longed for him to pin her against the food station and kiss her passionately. All she usually got was a whip of a tea towel across the leg, although he would always do it gently. She would watch the care and attention he put into his cooking and fantasised about it being a meal for just the two of them, over candlelight, which would end with him leading her up the stairs. That was her problem mainly. She believed in fairytales, but she had yet to play a part in one.

Her inner voice whispered, 'Come on, Stace, if you don't ask, you don't get.' She chewed the inside of her cheek and pulled her shoulders back. 'Steve, my mate Alice is coming in tonight and we are having some drinks. Why don't you join us after you knock off for the night?'

'Yeah sure. Sounds good.'

And that was it. She wasn't quite sure what to

make of his response. Maybe he hadn't realised she had just asked him out? Maybe he had and that was his reaction? Maybe he hadn't and wasn't interested in her? Either way, this was to be the first time they would spend time together without being paid to be there.

She smiled as she mopped the kitchen floor one last time. A warm feeling rushing through her.

'See you later, Steve,' she said quietly.

He echoed back without taking his eyes off the chicken livers he was preparing for his pate.

6

OLLIE

Ollie gazed across the water and watched the ripples as far out as they would go, letting his mind drift with the water. Netley was his favourite spot to come and be quiet and contemplate by the water. It soothed him. Even the discomfort from the stones underneath the blanket beneath him as he lay with his new Nikon D3500 couldn't distract him from the comfort of watching The Solent. The camera had cost him three-hundred and seventy-five pounds, which was the exact amount he had won in prize money for a photograph he had sent into a magazine. They had even written back to him saying that he had a great talent and that they would consider him for an apprentice-ship once he had finished school next year.

He was looking at the sailing boats gliding along, heading for The Isle of White, being tormented by the odd RIB weaving in and out. He wanted a candescent picture of a sailing boat in the sunset. RIBs did nothing for him. They were too hectic, dangerous, silly pieces of nautical design. For him, or at least for the sake of the photo he wanted, it had to be calm and elegant and silently strong.

He shuffled his body on the pebbled beach shore and dug down with his elbows. Click! He took the camera away from his face and squinted at the small digital screen before him. It was perfect. The orange sunset rippled on the sea intertwined with a royal blue. The sailing boat sitting neatly on top of calm water with a billowing sail. The crew mincing about like busy mice on board, preparing to take it down.

He loved looking at sailing boats. He considered them to be one of the finest pieces of manufacturing known to man. 'Are boats manufactured or engineered?' he wondered. 'Both, perhaps,' he concluded.

In a world of chaos, money, and technology, how brave must a person be to give it all up and surrender themselves to the sea, having faith in just a boat to keep them safe? But how utterly enthralling to take that risk too, he thought. As he stood up and packed away his things, he had decided that he should make sailing a hobby. He loved to watch; maybe he should get involved. In that moment he decided that next summer, once he had finished school and hopefully won some part-time photography work, he would try and get into sailing, or at least find out more about it. He loved the sea. Maybe it would love him.

He put his flask in his bag and looked at his phone. He had a message from Sky. She wanted to meet up. As the tide drew out, a wave of excitement came over him and he jumped up from his spot, suddenly full of energy and vigour. He had gotten the picture he wanted and now he had the company he wanted for the evening. Today had been a good day.

Once home, Ollie raced upstairs with heavy feet and chucked his school bag on his bedroom floor and it skimmed across the floor like a pebble across water.

He was giddy with excitement. He tried to brush off the questions feasting on his insecurities. *She probably only wants to hang out with you because everyone else is busy. She'll never go for a wimp like you. Guys like you don't get girls like her.* The insecurity monster was growing rapidly in size, but he kept humming to keep the noise and unwelcome parasite out.

He slapped on a bit of aftershave, followed by a swill of mouthwash. One quick glance in the mirror and he laughed to himself. *It'll never happen anyway, you goon.* He was laughing at his own thought, but for the first time in his life, he didn't care where it went. He just had to be with her.

He sped down the stairs and opened the front door with a startle.

'Sky? What are you doing here?'

'Umm ... we arranged to meet up,'—she looked at her watch—'about thirty minutes ago. You can't have forgotten already. I know you are not *that* stupid.'

Ollie's face flashed a bright shade of crimson. 'No, I just assumed I would come to yours. Girls shouldn't walk about on their own. It's not safe.'

'How about men stop raping women? Wouldn't that be a better argument?'

Ollie looked confused.

'Not you. Just rhetorically, you know? The news is always girls shouldn't wear this, girls shouldn't walk through parks alone, girls should watch their drinks. How about men just stop raping women? Why don't they say that?'

'Yeah. You make a good point, but that's like walking through a tiger enclosure with a piece of steak in your bag. I'm not saying it's right, but you will never be able to control people with a poisoned mind. You have to mitigate the risk.'

Sky was laughing.

'What?' retorted Ollie. 'It was the tiger analogy, wasn't it? Bollocks. I couldn't think of a good one on the spot. You know I will get one at 3 A.M. and text it to you, don't you?'

Sky fist-pumped Ollie and they walked aimlessly along the road. She was picking leaves off hedges and flicking them. Ollie couldn't get over how cool she was. She could even make hedge ripping and flicking look cool. He felt as though he could walk next to her forever as they meandered along the streets of Netley. Ollie occasionally bumped into her just so that he could brush his arm against her, getting a zap of electricity run through him every time he did, unbeknownst to her. She made him feel alive and yet she had no idea.

They reached the local fish-and-chip shop and Sky stopped to inhale the glorious fumes of chip-shop salt and vinegar emanating from the open door.

Ollie saw an opportunity. 'Are you hungry? Shall we get some food?' He gestured for her to go in front of him into the shop.

Sky looked at Ollie and squinted her eyes.

'What are you looking at me like that for? It's only a bag of chips.'

'Is it? I don't want to get your hopes up, Ollie.' Sky began to fidget slightly. She would never know from looking at him what a sledgehammer that was to his gut.

'I know.' Ollie pretended to laugh. 'It's a bag of chips, duh. Nothing more.'

'Yeah, but that whole wanting to collect me and

now offering to buy me food. It's a bit like, datey, isn't it?'

'Alright, love. Get over yourself. It's ... a ... bag ... of ... chips,' he said, dragging out his words as if she needed dumbing down, using humour as a defence.

Sky relaxed and gave a small giggle. 'Alright, then. My shout next time.'

Ollie was still standing by the door, allowing her to lead the way and quickly decided against that act of chivalry. He stepped forward to go first and they both clashed.

'Oi, watch it,' said Sky, playfully giving him a shove.

'Yeah, right. You don't get any special treatment from me. After all, I wouldn't want to be too *datey* now, would I?' he said mockingly.

They both laughed and made their way in.

A short while later, they both lay on the grass, looking up at the stars. Stuffed and greasy from their fish-and-chip take away.

'So, how come you moved then?'

'My parents, obviously.'

'Right.' Ollie didn't know what that meant and didn't know if he could ask more. 'So, when you say ...'

'My dad shagged the neighbour.'

'Oh ... I'm sorry. I shouldn't have asked.'

'Of course, you should've asked. It would be weirder if you didn't ask. Why do people say that these days?'

'Out of politeness, I guess.'

'We've got to always ask questions. It's up to me if I don't want to answer. A world without questions would be weird. Rather than asking people to be polite, why don't we ask people to expect questions? Sometimes, uncomfortable ones.'

'You have a lot of theories.'

'I call it common sense.'

'Have you thought about running for mayor?'

Sky gave Ollie a nudge in the ribs and they both laughed.

'So, come on then. Why do you get such a hard time at school?'

'Dunno really. It started years ago. Everyone latched on and it just became a way of life. I've accepted it for now, but I have big plans for adult me. Move away. Reinvent myself.'

'Is that right? Can I come?'

'Absolutely. But, Sky?'

'Yeah?'

'It's not a date, ok?'

They laughed loudly, and Sky rolled into Ollie, and he put an arm around her. The waxing moon was in full beam on the waterfront, leaving flashes of white on the navy water. This part of the park was Ollie's favourite and tonight it had become even more special. He knew Sky wasn't interested in him on any physical level, but he got the feeling he had just made his first friend for life. Fifteen years old and he had his first buddy. It made him want to shed a tear, but he was not going to do that. Not here. He gave her a squeeze and she exhaled deeply.

'BFFs," she whispered.

'BFFs,' he confirmed.

7

HANNAH

As Hannah kissed Craig goodbye at the front door, she knew it was over. She knew the dream she had been holding onto was gone. Her damp knickers told her that she was not pregnant. For some reason, she didn't want him to know. She couldn't face it. They had both been so sure this time. She had felt so different. She was tired. She was touchy. She just 'had that feeling' as all the mums had said in that stupid forum she had been using. She cursed herself for getting caught up in the excitement.

She waved Craig off and made sure he had gone before quickly opening her dressing gown and looking in her pants. She saw red. The period had arrived. It was the first time she had ever been late, but she could hardly say she had been pregnant. She had just been late.

She went into the downstairs shower room and took a proper look. The period, or possible miscarriage, had definitely arrived. Tears pricked her eyes, but they did not fall. The overwhelming numbness stopped that. She wished they would. It seemed as though this was the perfect time to cry and she felt frustrated that she couldn't even do that. She couldn't make a baby and she couldn't cry when it was completely appropriate to cry. She made her way into the kitchen, opened the fridge door, and took a swig of wine from an opened bottle. It was eight A.M.

She walked in a daze over to the sofa and slouched down into the corner of it, wishing it would suck her in to some kind of black hole. Suddenly, the quietness of the room became deafening. She didn't put the television on. She just stared out of the window. Her phone vibrated in her dressing gown pocket. She almost couldn't be bothered to look at it, but she did. It was Craig. He had sent her a message with the pregnant woman emoji and a love heart.

Her eyes pricked once more, but once again the tears were halted. This time by rage. She threw the phone across the floor and went back to the fridge for more wine. 'I'll stop at midday,' she told herself. No one was expecting her anywhere today. She could get drunk this morning and no one would be any the wiser by tea time. *Why not shake things up a bit? Who says you can only drink in the evenings? I bet heroin addicts don't wait until 5 P.M. I've lost a baby. I'm having a sodding drink.*

She grabbed some cheese and a packet of ham and closed the fridge with her elbow. Her morning plan had lifted her spirits. Now she knew she didn't have to be alone with her thoughts. She could use alcohol to numb her pain.

Halfway down the bottle of wine, she felt very woozy. The result seemed to be much more severe than if she had been evening drinking. She decided to seek comfort in the virtual world and logged on to the support group. She typed out a post and told them all she was having a miscarriage. The alcohol was talking now, and she was making quite the story out of how far gone she was, and the heartbreak that had followed. Craig didn't use social media, so she didn't care. She would never meet these people, so what did it matter if she expanded on the truth a little?

It wasn't long before she had several crying reactions and a multitude of care reactions on the post. The messages began coming in too. These people she had never met all wanted to check in and offer their support. They had all been there. All bar one.

All the names in her inbox had been female until AnonymousDaddy caught her attention. She clicked to open the message.

'Hi, I saw your sad news. Sorry for your loss. I can help and have helped many others like you. I donate sperm. I have been doing it for years with a 95% success rate in fertile women. I would be happy to try with you. Real father does not need to know. I am clean. I don't want payment. I just ask that I have sex with you to make it happen. It's not for everyone, so if I offended you say no. On the other hand, you might just enjoy it. AD'

Hannah had to almost scrape her jaw off the floor. She could not believe what she was reading. *What a pervert. Sicko!* Her mind was racing as to who would actually go along with something like that. Then he sent a picture. It was of him holding his penis. You couldn't see his face, but you could see a very ripped torso and his very large cock. Hannah could not stop looking at it. She came out of the message and closed the app.

The message from AnonymousDaddy had put her off her wine, which was clearly a good thing. She got dressed and after necking a glass of water, decided to go for a walk with Rosie. As she ambled along the country lanes with her pooch, she wondered what it would be like to be pushing a pushchair. She loved walking her dog. She felt like she was a proud dog owner and enjoyed saying hello to other dog walkers on her travels. The dog community was strong, and she smiled to herself at the thought of saying hello to other parents.

Back at the house, she still couldn't get her head around what had happened that morning. She almost laughed to herself as she shook her head in disbelief. Peeling off her sweaty clothes and loading the washing machine, she emptied the pockets on Craig's trousers and found a receipt. She was about to toss it in the bin but decided to look at it. Two starters, two mains, a bottle of red and one dessert. It was from that new French place up the road, the one she had been saying she wanted to go to for weeks. A wave of heat ran over her from her head right down to her toes. Her mind began piecing together possible scenarios as her head pulsated with disbelief and rage. She looked at it. And then looked again. She checked the date and then she looked at the date in her phone and checked through her messages. He had been playing tennis that afternoon, and then went for a pub dinner with Matt.

Bastard. She crumpled up the receipt and shoved it into the bin and marched through to the shower room. She turned the shower on full blast and got into it, desperately wanting to wash away her grief. Now, she cried. The tears that had been building up had finally burst out of her eyes and she felt them stream down her face as the blood streamed down between her legs. She sobbed and sobbed and sobbed. She had lost everything.

After howling out her pain in private, she got out, and patted her face dry, and looked at herself in the mirror. She was exhausted.

Get a grip Hannah. Do not let him get away with this. This is revenge.

Hannah had a plan and it started with a romantic night for two and keeping quiet until her next ovulation window.

8

ALICE

The nights were beginning to get warmer and longer. A variety of snowdrops and daffodils were beginning to make an appearance along the narrow path that Alice was wandering along. Life was good. She hadn't spoken to Dan in a few weeks now and she had once again, started taking care of herself. Rather than try and take up old habits that had failed (the gym), she joined a yoga class instead. It had been refreshing. Alcohol and yoga were not exactly a match and she had enjoyed getting to know, ok, smiling politely and gesturing a quiet 'hi' to her classmates. These people seemed to have their shit together. They were not craving drama, chaos, or attention. In fact, it was the opposite. It was peaceful. It was respectful, and it was purely for the benefit of the user.

She had been going for three weeks now and hadn't drank during that time either. She'd been invited out numerous times but had feigned illness to get out of awkward social situations. She still wasn't sure if she was a fully-fledged alcoholic or just someone who'd lost their way for a while. She did know, however, that she was not about to test that theory. She knew she could not yet be trusted around alcohol. Addressing her issues with alcohol had been toilsome and she was not about to ruin what she had achieved so far.

Every day or evening now, she found herself expressing gratitude or finding the joy in simple things. Take tonight for example, walking along the path where Spring had sprung; she loved the way Spring flowers were symbolic of new beginnings. The harsh winters killed off outdoor life, but Spring would come and bring newness and colour. It was a ray of hope, coming from the flowerbeds. When she was a possible alcoholic, she thought people that enjoyed simple things were sad. People that commented on the view or remarked on the delights of daffodils and such were losers. She concluded that they must never have been hurt to be able to find joy in such simple things. Now, she was learning that maybe they had been hurt the most and had had to rebuild their lives. Of course, there would be some who had led peaceful lives. Not everyone had to experience misery to become kind. Some were blessed from the onset with a good nature, she concurred.

Alice stopped and looked around. The sun was beginning to set. The air had a pleasant chill about it. The street lamp pinged into light and gave clues and yet hid secrets. She knelt down and picked up a collection of daffodils. They were bright and velvety to touch. She had a napkin in her kitbag and used it to tightly wrap the stems of the bundle and put them neatly away. Pausing to take one more look around and enjoy the evidence of Spring, she went about the rest of her walk home, enjoying seeing her hot breath leave her mouth in the chilly Spring time air.

Once home, Alice dumped her kitbag on the floor in the hallway and went upstairs and began a bath, to which she added some salts. She sat on the edge, watching the water pour in ferociously from the taps. She found herself daydreaming and slipped into thoughts of alcohol. Standing up, she shook her body like a wet dog and went into her bedroom and immediately started doing press-ups, trying to banish the desire to drink. *Why does something that takes so much never lose its appeal? God dammit.*

She jolted up and thought about the misery an alcohol binge would bring and the pure organic joy that came from exercise ... and yet all she could picture was how this bath was missing a glass of a crisp white Sauvignon Blanc sitting on the side, coated in condensation from the heat in the bathroom.

The thoughts began to creep in. The battle began. Urges running through her. *You've been so good recently. You deserve it. Three weeks is great. You're not an alcoholic. You were going through a bad time. You're better now. You don't have to have the whole bottle. Just have one glass. Yes. Do that. Buy a bottle, but just have one glass. You can do that. Treat yourself.*

'Fuck sake.'

She threw on a jumper, ran downstairs, and grabbed her car keys. It had taken her less time to drive to the garage, grab a bottle of her 'favourite' wine, and drive back home again than it did to run a bath. She smuggled it in as if she had just scored heroin or something, terrified that one of her neighbours would be outside and start chatting the time of day with her. She had no time for idle chat now.

Once inside, she cracked open the bottle, and took a swig straight from it. It was as if the swig of wine put out fires that had been simmering away, never quite going out, and suddenly she felt relaxed. She put the lid back on the bottle and looked at it on the side.

'Alice, put it in the fridge. You are the boss and you don't need more. The itch has been scratched.' She bit her lip, put it in the fridge, and made her way up the stairs. She made it up halfway before turning back, running back down, opening the fridge, pouring almost as much as a large wine glass could take, and retreating to the steam-filled bathroom.

The shrill beeping of the alarm clock ringing in her ears woke Alice from the deep sleep that she was in. Pulling the pillow over her head in an attempt to stifle the noise, she rolled onto her front. Her head was already throbbing with pain without the noise of the alarm. She tried to smack the alarm off by whacking it with her arm, but she knocked it over instead and it landed on the floor, forcing her to roll over to the other side of the bed and retrieve it. She turned it off and tossed it on to the bedside table.

Begrudgingly, she lifted her legs out of the bed and sat upright, stretching herself awake. She was bitterly disappointed in the 'winecident' the night before and battled for several minutes in her head about going for a run. It was the last thing she felt like doing but she knew he had to. She owed it to herself.

The morning air was crisp and dewy. It wasn't complete daylight yet, but it almost was. It was the time of year where it seemed as if everyone should still be asleep because of the dark mornings. Kitchen lights glowing on the pavement and gas fumes venting out of houses, letting you know that was not the case. The streets that were silent just a few hours ago were slowly waking up and bringing life back once again.

Alice began a light jog and knew it wouldn't be a long one this time, but something was better than nothing. About one and a half miles into it, something startled her. Dan's car. He didn't have any friends around here. Immediately she knew he must be with a woman and the little breath she had left escaped her. She jogged closer to see if she could see anything. She didn't know what she was looking for—*anything*. A sign. Evidence. A light flicked on upstairs and Alice bolted.

Once Alice returned home, having cut short her run, she couldn't stop thinking of Dan. She was irritated by both of those things. She had been happy recently and hadn't given him much thought. Now, she couldn't get him out of her head, and she was obsessing over who he had spent the night with.

9

OLLIE

Life had been good for Ollie recently. It was almost a foreign feeling and he was enjoying it so much that he was scared it would end. Happy anxiety. It wouldn't be a feeling of Ollie's if it didn't come with some level of anxiety.

His blossoming friendship with Sky was gathering pace. They spent most weeknights together now. She had introduced him to comic books and grunge music. He had even put on some black eyeliner recently in the privacy of his own house and quite liked it. He wiped it off before anyone else got to know about it though. He was not brave enough to showcase that look just yet.

Sky was transforming him in more mays than one. He had a new outlook on life. Suddenly, he had a zest for life. He looked forward to going to school for the first time in his memory. The bullies had started to back off too. They daren't say anything to him when he was with Sky.

Sky took school work seriously and now Ollie started applying himself too as they sat together in all of their lessons. She could never understand why the 'cool' kids thought it was 'cool' not to learn. What wasn't impressive about knowing stuff, she told Ollie. He had never really given it much thought, but now he wanted to know everything. The more stuff he knew, the more he would have to talk to Sky about. What impressed him even more was that she showed an interest in his photography and started joining him on his little local adventures to find interesting things to take photos of.

One evening, whilst she was sitting in her bed and he lay on her bedroom floor, she got out a map of the region and circled places they could visit to broaden his portfolio. He loved her interest in his hobby and her desire to help him expand on it. It had never occurred to him to explore the surrounding region. He had always kept himself to himself through fear of running into the bullies. You couldn't escape them on trains and on buses he concluded, so he had avoided them and eliminated all risk.

Since Sky had been working on his photography with him, the amount of likes he was getting on Instagram was up too. He couldn't figure out what he was doing differently, but he was getting noticed by people in different countries around the globe. Life was good, and he was finally beginning to enjoy it.

After a sunny but fresh afternoon down by the waterfront, taking pictures of boats and of Sky, they packed up their things and headed back to Ollie's. He had suggested that they watch a film and he could make some cheesy nachos and she had agreed. He loved being in her company. She was so easy-going. They always had fun, they had plenty to talk about, and she was so interesting. She was really into music, and she had introduced him to lots of new bands and songs he had never heard before.

Ollie was in awe of her. Had she always been this cool, he wondered. Everywhere she went, every person she encountered, he could see that everyone must've loved her. She was the kind of girl that was impossible not to love. At least that was what he thought. Goosebumps tickled his arms and he looked round at her, paying close attention to her mouth. A thought entered his mind about what it would be like to kiss her, but he banished it as quickly as he could, reminding himself never to cross that line. She had made it clear that she was not interested, and he would never want to risk what he had with her now.

Ollie turned the key in the lock of his front door and was in mid-conversation with Sky when he saw his mother laying lifeless on the floor in the kitchen diner. He dropped his bags and speedily made his way in with Sky, close behind him. His mother was lying there with blood coming from her head and seemed to be unconscious.

'She must've been wasted.' He held his fingers to her neck and was relieved to find a pulse.

Sky was calling an ambulance. Ollie looked more closely at his mother and realised this was not a cracked head. He knelt and examined her closely, gently sweeping away her thick dark hair that was soaked in blood and could see that this looked like a severe head injury.

'I think we need to call the police too.' He began pacing the kitchen, struggling to concentrate as a huge knot of anxiety formed in his stomach and the panic began to sweat out of him.

Sky looked at him and nodded to what was behind him. The back door out of the kitchen was ajar and there was broken crockery on the floor. Her bag was on the side and her purse was open. There was no money in it but that wasn't particularly unusual.

The next hour passed in a haze as the paramedics arrived and stretchered his mother away. He and Sky were allowed to accompany her in the ambulance as the police got on with their work in the property. They said they would meet Ollie at the hospital in a short while for further questions. The two teenagers were silent for the duration of the journey, but Sky leaned in to Ollie and held his hand. He had never felt so loved, despite a feeling of ambivalence in the situation he found himself in. He was happier about Sky holding his hand than any other feelings he had, such as concern for his mother, and that made him question his own mind for a moment. The guilt at his own happiness to be holding hands with Sky, which was happening because his mother had been assaulted. He pushed that thought to the back of his head and locked it away in a drawer.

The police confirmed that his mother had been struck with a blunt force object, which had resulted in a bleed on the brain. She was put into a medically-induced coma for her best chance of survival. The commotion of the last couple of hours had segregated the seriousness of the situation for Ollie. He had assumed that because she had a pulse she was going to be ok. It hadn't crossed his mind that she might not be out of the woods yet. He started to feel guilty about the joy he felt from holding Sky's hand when his mother was fighting for her life on a stretcher, being blue-lighted to emergency care in front of him. Again, he began to question his own character at that thought and a tear escaped the wall of his eye socket and trickled down his cheek. It landed on Sky's hand, which was still wrapped tightly around his.

The policeman was talking but Ollie could hardly make sense of it. His ears swam in white noise. Images of them being happy just a few hours beforehand ... to then finding his mother on the floor half-dead.

Sky unclasped her hand and looked at him. 'It's important, Ollie. Can you think of anyone who would want to do this to her?'

Ollie stood up and put both his hands on the back of his head. 'I don't know her.' His chin quivered as he started to give in to a tidal wave of emotion rising within. 'She ... she was an alcoholic. We ... we barely spoke these days.' Another tear fell. 'I don't know if she had a boyfriend. The last few have been pretty grim, so I have kept out of it. There may have been drugs. I don't know. I don't know her. I don't know my own mother.'

The tidal wave of tears had now reached the eyes and, unable to hold them back, they poured over his eyelashes like mini waterfalls. He struggled to breathe, and Sky grabbed him and hugged him so tightly that she was going to stop him from breathing. He hardly had the strength to stand as Sky guided him back to his seat, where he almost flopped down.

The policeman gave Sky a concerned smile. 'Does he have anywhere to go tonight?'

'He can stay with me. He can stay with me for as long as he likes.'

The policeman gave them both a lift back to Sky's house. There was nothing else that could be done at the hospital and the staff encouraged Ollie to go and get some rest and promised to keep him updated. The police officer kept glancing into his rearview mirror and watched how emotionally mature Sky was with Ollie. He thought it seemed almost like a mother and child embrace and sensed without doubt that Ollie had been starved of love whilst growing up. The nights like this were tough. Seeing people physically ache through love and fear. If only his job consisted of petty criminals, or if only he could mend a neglected teenager's heart. 'It never gets any easier,' he muttered to himself.

They pulled up outside a large detached Edwardian house. It had a gravel drive with a small roundabout in it. They had to buzz in from the other side of the electric gates. The front entrance was extended and held up with Roman-style white pillars. Along the front of the property were spotlights in the ground, lighting up each sash window.

Sky's mother came to the entrance and was a dazzling image of African beauty. Her shoulder-length afro was almost wider than her shoulders. She was tall and slender, and wearing a long black maxi dress that slightly hugged her hips. She had lots of tasteful bohemian jewellery on and didn't look old enough to be Sky's mother, but only by appearance. Her eyes belonged to a very wise woman, and she was older than her years emotionally.

Sky shuffled in with Ollie and took him into the back lounge. The house was mainly white and beige, with silver and grey furnishings. Ollie sat down on the velour chesterfield and stared into space.

'I'll go and get you a drink.' Sky looked at him, but he was zoning out. She went and met her mother at the door, who was getting the last of the details from the policeman.

'Before I go, I will just add what a lovely young lady you have raised for a daughter. I can only imagine this night would've been very different for him had he not got a friend like her. She's very wise and mature.'

Sky's mum blushed and thanked him.

The moonlit sky started to spit with rain. It looked like tiny flecks of snow under the outdoor spotlights. The policeman got back in his car with a deep sigh. The electric gates opened to let him out and the outdoor spotlights went off.

10

HANNAH

It had been a very challenging two weeks for Hannah. She didn't want Craig to know she had found the receipt. She couldn't be sure it was deceit either, but it certainly didn't look good. She dropped into conversation a couple of times about the French restaurant and saying she really wanted to go, but Craig dismissed it the first time and the second time he told her he had heard it was rubbish. Overpriced and small portions. They hadn't had sex and he was spending more time at the tennis club and hanging out with 'Matt'.

She was determined to win whatever this situation was. She wanted a baby. She had a husband. He had a low sperm count. She noticed how he had been drinking more than normal recently, which wasn't going to help their fertility issues, but who was she to complain? She was drinking a lot more than she should be too.

Over the last two weeks, she had been making more of an effort with her appearance, which had gone unnoticed. She had cooked nicer dinners, most of which had been left to reheat later because Craig was home late.

Here she was again, dressed up, wearing his favourite perfume, and waiting for him when the text came: 'Leave mine in the oven, I'm just having one more tennis match.'

She threw her phone across the floor and let out a frustrated scream. Fists clenched, she started pacing. The table was laid beautifully again, but like her, it was dressed to party with no one to host. She blew out the candles and grabbed her car keys.

Her heart was racing as she headed for the tennis club. She was scared of what she might find. What if she saw him with a woman? What if she saw he was with Matt and wasn't cheating on her? What if he wasn't there? As she approached the tennis club, she realised how ridiculous she was being, and probably wasn't going to find anything. She planned to turn around in the car park and head home before he spotted her and made a scene.

She drove in and went to the end of the car park where it wasn't lit. Just as she was about to pull away, she saw him ... he was with Matt. The tension in her body simmered down and suddenly she felt really silly. She sat there silently, lights off, engine off. She would have to wait or him to leave; otherwise, he would see her. She watched him and Matt high-five each other and share a fist pump. It looked as though Craig had won the match this time. Her heart sank a little. Craig was a good guy. She had been putting so much pressure on him to have a baby. He must have been feeling like it was his fault with the low sperm count. They had never really discussed how he felt about it.

He got in his car, and she could see the light from his phone glowing on his face. He was sitting there, texting. She just wanted him to hurry up and leave so she could go home and put this episode at the back of her mind. She would have to make a detour to the shop and buy something to add to their meal to explain why she had left in a hurry.

The lights at the tennis club went off and he started up his car. Hannah let out a sigh of relief. His lights went on. A young woman locked the tennis club doors and walked in front of his car. She got in and now they were kissing. Hannah watched in horror.

The woman can't have been more than twenty-one. She had long brown hair and was very petite. Her husband *was* having an affair and with a woman that was barely an adult. She wanted to start her car and drive into them, but she was so shocked, she was frozen to her seat. She watched as he had his hands in her hair and was kissing her passionately. He hadn't kissed her like that in a very long time. *How long has this been going on for? Does Matt know? Are they both laughing at me?*

Craig finally untangled himself from his lover and drove off. Hannah wiped away the tears that flowed uncontrollably and drove herself home.

As she put the key in the lock, she opened the front door to what no longer felt like home. It felt like a set. A set from the sitcom which was her life. There she had been, cooking, cleaning, dressing up, trying ... always trying, and for what? To be lied to. To be deceived. To be disrespected. To be devalued. To be cheated on. To be denied the loyalty that they'd vowed to each other.

She slowly made her way into the kitchen. Picking up the pot of simmering Bolognese, she tipped it into the bin, including the pan. She cleared the table and did the washing up on auto. It was as if she were in a trance. She was numb. She couldn't get rid of the image of seeing her husband kissing that girl. That barely legal woman.

After quickly drinking several glasses of wine, she slumped on the sofa and got out her iPad. She logged on to her social media account and went to take solace in other people's misery. On the mums-to-be group she had joined, there were lots of posts from women who had successfully conceived, sharing scan photos or artistic announcement photos. Low didn't come close to how she was feeling right now. She had no baby. Her husband was cheating on her. She just wanted something to go her way. And then she remembered. Anonymous Daddy. She hovered the arrow over the messages' icon. Taking a deep breath, she opened his message and read it again. Then she typed.

'I'm ready to meet. Can we get together tomorrow?' Her heart was racing. She couldn't believe her own thoughts. She gulped back her wine and saw he was replying. She immediately sat bolt upright and fixated on the screen.

'Yes. Would love to. What time suits and where?'

'I'll book us a room somewhere. How about 10 A.M. at the Waverley? I will book a room under 'Collins'. Please delete this message thread.'

'See you there. Here is a picture of me.'

He was much better looking than she had expected and suddenly there were butterflies in her stomach. She had never done anything remotely dangerous before. Suddenly, she felt more alive than ever.

————

Craig opened the door quietly and came in to find Hannah asleep on the sofa. Her iPad was on her lap and an empty wine glass on the floor near her arm, which was hanging over the edge. She heard him come in but pretended to be asleep. She wanted to see if he would try to wake her. He didn't. She heard him go into the kitchen and decided to confront him.

'Hey. You're late.'

'And you're drunk. Again.'

'I'm not. I just had a couple. The wine is my company when you are not around. What have you been up to?'

'Nothing.'

'Well, you must've been doing something. It's 9.30 P.M.'

'Just food with Matt after tennis.'

'Matt sees more of you than I do at the moment. Don't you want to be here anymore?'

He paused. 'Of course, I do. Sorry, honey. I just needed to de -stress after work.' He walked over to her.

'You want me, don't you?' He pulled her in and swept her hair away from her eyes. 'Even after all these years ... I've still got it, haven't I?'

A rage began to simmer within her.

'You know you do, baby. So, umm ... I'm ovulating.'

He paused again. Poured himself a glass of wine and knocked it back.

'Are you now? Well ... what are we waiting for?'
He took her by the hand and led her upstairs.

11

ALICE

A week had passed since Alice had seen Dan's car parked just a few short streets away from where she lived. She spent the day after trying to keep as busy as possible, followed by an evening of breaking her sobriety to numb the pain. Loving a man like that and separating from a man like that had been like nothing she had ever experienced before. He was cold.

She had thought back to when they met. How interested he was in her. How he hung off every word she said. The hour-long phone calls. The endless texts. The gifts. The waking up early together so they could have sex before work. The cooking together in the evening. They never watched TV. They had wine and talked. The Dan she'd recently split from was miles apart. He was moody, sulky, and not interested in her. It hurt her a lot because she was still heavily invested in him and hated to see him disappearing in front of her. He was like a candle at the end of its burn time. A small flame, dancing for its last hour before the candle was no more. She was the flame flickering so desperately to stay alight, yet the candle offered her nothing left to burn.

That's why they fought so much in the end. Alice knew when they had spent time together that he hadn't wanted her there. She annoyed him. He would ask her to talk quietly. He didn't listen to what she was saying to him and would give the wrong answers because of that. He was just using her for sex and she knew it. It hurt, but it hurt even more that she went along with it, hoping the old Dan would reappear.

When they had finally split, she felt relief along with disappointment. She realised he had gone. The old Dan had gone, and he was not coming back. Was the Dan she'd met even real, she pondered. Was it all an act?

Had she fallen in love with someone who didn't even exist? What did that mean for how she was feeling now? Was she grieving for someone completely made up? Not the recent Dan who made her lose her mind and turn her towards a slippery slope of alcoholic binges and regrettable behaviour.

She was getting her life back on track. The yoga was great. Eating healthily was great. Seeing friends again who were delighted that Dan was gone was helpful. Seeing his car at that house last week had been a setback but only a minor one. She let him ruin her when they were together. She was not going to let him ruin her when they weren't together.

This time he was empowering her. She started running every morning. She hadn't run this much since she was a teenager. So what if it was to run past that house and look for his car each day? It was motivating. She hadn't, admittedly, seen his car since and that kept her spirits up. She didn't want him back, but she also did not want him falling in love and being the 'great Dan' she met living just around the corner.

Alice had a plan of action. Since giving up the booze and doing regular exercise, she was motivated and focussed. She had cut out pictures of women she wanted to look like and stuck them on her fridge. She wanted to get fit and have a style overhaul. She needed to start feeling good about herself, and that meant not regurgitating the same looks she'd worn with Dan. She was going to become someone she was proud of. She was going to be reborn.

Then she was going to meet the man of her dreams who would never fall out of love with her or lose interest because she would be interesting. The new man would be a bit older, mature with lots of life experience to share over candlelit dinners. He would be big and strong yet sweet and kind. He would stroke her hair on the sofa, hold her hand in the street. He'd rush home to see her after a long day at work and they would wake up in each other's arms in the morning. They would have romantic holidays abroad and take silly snaps of themselves trying to feed each other the local cuisine, and upload to Facebook and they'd get loads of likes. People would comment, saying how happy she looked and how lucky he was. He would love her friends and she would love his. When she met his, they'd say how glad they were to finally see him with a nice girl and her friends would say they no longer had to worry about her now that the gentle giant was here.

They would thank him for making her so happy. New Year's Eve would be a special night because it would be the night he would propose after an eight-month whirlwind romance. She would look lovingly into his eyes after they had kissed and wonder why the hell she had ever lost sleep over Dan?

12

OLLIE

Sky's mother and Sky had shown Ollie more love and compassion in the last forty-eight hours than he had ever felt in his life. Even the tiny things. On the first morning he woke up, Sky had brought him a cup of hot sweet tea in bed and her mother had come in a short while after with a large fluffy towel that she had warmed in the tumble dryer for him before urging him to take a long hot shower or bath, whichever he preferred, and promised him it would help him prepare for whatever the day threw at him.

Ollie smiled and accepted the towel and thought how wonderful it must be to grow up in a home where people warmed your towels and made you cups of tea.

Later that morning, he made his way to the hospital to see his mother. Sky was by his side. They hadn't discussed it. She was just there, and he felt like he could handle this with her next to him. If he had been alone, he would've been scared and fearful of what the coming days might bring. With her presence, he was able to rationalise his feelings. With her there, he felt stronger.

He sat by his mother's side and held her hand. It was lifeless. It felt strange to grip someone's hand and to not get a squeeze back.

Sky watched him intently. 'What are you thinking?'

'Honestly? I'm thinking where will I live if she dies. Does that make me a terrible person?'

'No. It makes you normal. Grief gets in the way of processing things in order. She's still here so you aren't grieving her. How can you know how you will feel if she goes? You can't. Keep worrying about somewhere to live; it will give you focus.'

'You're so smart. Among other things.' Ollie looked at Sky, completely enamoured by her grace and maturity.

The doctors came and explained that Ollie's mother was not in a good way. Her injury was bad enough on its own, but her body was weak from the alcohol and drug abuse. They prepared him for the fact that she might not make it. Then his real emotions came, and he now understood Sky's comment. He couldn't care less where he lived now; all he could think about was losing his mum and he knew Sky had been trying to prevent that for him. She put an arm around him, and he buried into her and sobbed.

As they got up to leave, he squeezed his mother's hand again, and he could've sworn he felt a tiny squeeze back. He gleefully told the nurse on the way out and she curled an inward smile at him. He knew what she was thinking, and his hopeful thinking slowly slipped away as his heart sank.

Back at Sky's house, she made him lay on the sofa with a blanket and said they would watch a film. She made him a bowl of chicken soup and served it with crusty bread.

'Eat.'

Ollie went to put up his hand.

'Eat. I won't take no for an answer.'

He pulled himself into an upright position and accepted the soup.

'Chicken soup is good for the soul, so good in fact, that there is even a book called that.'

Sky put a film on the television and Ollie couldn't quite process what he was experiencing. A few miles down the road, his mother was fighting for her life after being attacked in her own home, most likely by someone she knew. And here he was living in the lap of luxury, being cared for by the woman of his dreams. This house looked like something straight out of a magazine. Every last detail, from light fittings to sheepskin rugs to candles, to fake flowers, to full length mirrors, and intriguing artwork. One thing was for sure: he was so glad to be here rather than in his box bedroom with wood-chip wallpaper and mould around the window.

A short while later, the phone rang. Sky's mother glided into the room like some kind of angel, peacefully and beautifully. 'Ollie, it's for you. The hospital.'

Ollie gulped and looked at Sky. She nodded at him and put her hand on his knee as her mother passed him the phone. Ollie nodded, gulped a few more times, and said 'ok' before ending the call.

'Is it time to go?' Sky's mother asked quietly and delicately.

Ollie nodded, fighting back the tears.

'I'll get our coats.' She left the room, again so quietly you couldn't hear her footsteps on the ground.

The three of them drove to the hospital without speaking. Ollie watched suburbia pass by him out of the window whilst visions of his mother drunk and arguing with him danced around in his head. He began to wonder if he could've helped her. All that time he spent in his room avoiding her, scared of her ... he knew he was not equipped to offer her any support. She was far too gone into the world of addiction before he was old enough to really understand it.

He was snatched out of his sombre thoughts by Sky opening his door. They had reached the hospital and he hadn't even realised. He looked up at her and it took everything in her to give him a smile, rather than look away from her friend's heartbreak. She offered him her hand and helped hoist him out of the car.

Sky's mum came around from her side of the car and put his face in both of her hands. 'Whatever happens, we will help you. Don't worry about anything else right now. It's time to say goodbye and you have got us.'

Ollie's chin wobbled. He took as deep a breath as he could muster, and his voice cracked as he exhaled. The three of them walked in to the hospital in a line.

13

HANNAH

Hannah waited for the click of the front door closing to confirm Craig had left for work. As soon as she heard his car start up outside, she ran to the en suite and lunged forward on the sink, wishing she could be sick. She hadn't eaten since before arriving at the tennis club the night before, so there was nothing to throw up now. She raised her head and looked at herself with disgust in the bathroom mirror. Did she know the woman staring back at her? This woman was so desperate for a baby that she had sex with her husband just hours after seeing him kiss another woman. After months of telling her she was insecure, she was going mad, she was making things up ... she saw the proof that none of that was true ... and then had sex with her husband.

Not only was he a cheater, he was a coercive controlling monster. Who said those kind of things to a woman? If he was really good at lying, he could've said, 'Baby, what's going on? Why are you feeling like that? How can I help?' instead of 'You're losing it. You're imagining things. You are so insecure.'

Not only was he betraying her physically, he was betraying her emotionally.

She jumped in the shower and in a rushed job, got herself clean as best and as quickly as she could. She had a very important appointment of her own today.

She scanned her wardrobe for the perfect outfit. *Casual? Or power woman?* Who knew what the right thing to wear was to this kind of meeting? Part of her thought to dress pretty low-key and casual, in case she was spotted. The other part of her thought this was a brand new experience and one she was never likely to do again, so she should dress to the nines. She eventually opted for something in between.

She took one last glance in the mirror before she left and thought she looked a bit like Princess Diana. She was wearing tight, high-waisted white jeans and a white-and-black bodysuit revealing her very ample bosom, and a black blazer emblazoned with big gold buttons. Her hair was blown out and she sported clip-on earrings ... she did have a duchess look about her. One thing that could be said was that it was highly unlikely that any aristocratic woman would ever become entangled in this kind of indecent proposal.

She hopped into her car and drove to the train station just a couple of miles down the road. From there she abandoned her car and called a taxi. Looking around her, making sure she didn't see anyone she knew, she hurriedly got into the taxi and told the driver to take her to The Waverley Hotel. On the way there, she called the hotel.

'Hello, yes I have a booking with you for one evening. I was wondering what the earliest time would be that my room is ready, and if I can make a booking at the spa.'

The receptionist told her they had some rooms made up already and that there were spaces in the spa from the afternoon.

'Fabulous. I will be with you shortly and would like to check in right away please, and I'd like a Swedish massage around 12.30. Thank you. See you shortly.' She ended the call and opened her messages. 'The room and I will be waiting for you by 10.30. I'll send you the number once I have checked in.' Message sent. Her heart skipped a beat and she started to feel hot. She opened the window just a little and as the cool breeze skimmed her face, she smirked. The power was all hers.

Hannah channelled every ounce of nervous energy she had in to dominating this arrangement. She was petrified. This was like something out of a movie. No one else she knew had ever done something like this. No one she knew would suspect *her* for doing something like this. She couldn't think about it. She couldn't entertain the risk or the danger. This was a role she was going to play. Surely it would be one hour of her life. One hour of acting. If she could get through that, then she had the rest of the day to herself. The rest of the day to enjoy the spa, have room service, and relax. She was going to embrace the lunacy. This was a one-time thing ...

There was a knock at the door. She leapt off the bed and took a quick look at herself in the full-length mirror. The short satin dressing gown she had taken from home was just covering her bum and was gaping open at the front, just about keeping her breasts inside. Her hair looked great, her make-up was untouched, and her lips painted a raspberry pink.

'This is it,' she whispered to herself and took a deep breath.

She tiptoed to the door and looked through the peephole. All she could see was a close-up of his shirt. He was tall, that was a good thing, she told herself. His shirt looked like a nice one. Shoulders back. One more deep breath ...

Very slowly she opened the door, hiding herself behind it, and craning her neck around. 'Hello ... Anonymous Daddy ...'

She was taken aback by his Italian looks. Dark hair. Broad shoulders. A very prominent jaw. He was better looking than Craig. She could hardly believe her luck. Her inner voice quickly reminded her that he went around the city having sex with desperate women for free because they wanted babies. He was hardly the catch, a freak even, but he would do nicely for today. She went to speak and he put his finger to her mouth and shook his head. She nodded back.

He held up a piece of paperwork in front of her. It was a sexual health screening report. He pointed to the date. It was dated yesterday. He threw it on the floor and grabbed her and kissed her hard, one hand on the back of her head, one on the small of her back, pulling her in tightly.

She was scared and yet buzzing with excitement. She found herself kissing him back and lifting one leg up and wrapping it around him. He took his hand from her head, pulled back, and sucked his finger whilst holding her stare, and then went underneath her gown and between her legs.

She let out a slight whimper and he kissed her neck. He pushed her onto the bed, ripping open her gown, and began kissing her, and started making his way down. She wriggled and writhed with every touch he made, every kiss he planted, every lick he gave. She was euphoric. He was ravenous. He quickly undid his shirt, kissing and licking her between each button. Off came his trousers and she looked whilst panting heavily ... he was big. Bigger than Craig. He pushed himself inside her. She groaned loudly, and he growled like a tiger which made her laugh and pull him in deeper.

One hour later, and after a short nap together, she was lying in bed; the reality of what had happened started to unfold. He was doing up his shirt. They still had not spoken. She didn't know if she should. She felt that it seemed odd not to, but all this had ever been was an arrangement. She stretched her toes out from beneath the covers and stroked his hip, barely able to reach. He paused doing up his buttons and looked at her. Their eyes locked. He bit his lip. She bit hers back and he pounced back on her, kissing her hard.

This time she rolled on top of him and took charge. She pushed back his shoulders into the bed and arched her back on top of him. He grabbed her breasts. She ran her hand through her hair whilst rocking back and forth on him. He sat up, holding on to her and swinging her beneath him. He pushed hard into her and then slowly back out. He pulled her around and pushed her face into the pillow. She pushed back on to him. Tightly, he held on to her hips.

They were moaning together, louder and louder, faster and deeper, until finally they both let out one long groan in unison, him still holding her hips against him as she shook with pleasure. Slowly, she collapsed onto the bed and he on top of her. Giving her one final slow thrust as he emptied himself into her. He kissed her neck. She stroked his leg. Still, they had not spoken to each other, and he pulled out, got up and made his way into the shower.

Perhaps she should let him go? She decided to say nothing. She watched him dress. He watched her as she watched him. The silence deafening. It was as if they were both desperate to say something and yet neither of them did. Hannah felt alive. It was the best sex she had had in months, maybe longer. As for Anonymous Daddy, he had never seen a woman enjoy him so much in this predicament. Normally, it was a business transaction, and they were nervous. He saw Hannah come alive. She wanted him, and he wanted her. He loved watching her enjoy every moment. She performed for him instead of the other way around. Part of him wondered if he would ever see her again. Part of him wanted to.

Just like that. The Anonymous Daddy had come (literally) and gone. He was hot. He was the best sex she had ever had, and he had gone. She lay there and began to laugh ... and then she laughed more and more and more. She was in hysterics. He might have made her pregnant and she didn't have a single care in the world. She decided to have one celebratory glass of champagne. She helped herself from the mini bar, completely elated at the complete power trip she had just been through, and as she brought the flute to her lips, she whispered, 'Fuck you, Craig. Fuck you.'

That afternoon, Hannah enjoyed an aromatherapy massage. When filling out the consultation form, there was a box that asked to be ticked if there was a chance you could be pregnant. She left it blank.

Surely it's safe to have a massage on day one? Plus, it might not have worked. I might not be pregnant.

Today was her last day of treats for the next two weeks whilst she played the waiting game. She had had her glass of celebratory champagne, she had had a massage, and now she was enjoying the jacuzzi. All the things that would have to stop if she was pregnant.

She told Craig she was visiting and staying with her friend that night. She knew he wouldn't care. She then realised he would probably spend the night with his new young lover, which smarted a bit. Her mind began to wander, and she imagined what it might be like to invite her secret lover back for the night. Images and visions of the duvet being thrown off the bed, her legs in the air and his dark, muscly back going up and down on her, which she could see in the mirror behind him.

That afternoon she read the remaining half of her book in one sitting. She was relaxed, she felt content, and as long as she didn't think about what Craig could be doing, she felt completely at one with herself. She didn't feel an ounce of guilt over what she had done. She felt empowered. She felt courageous. She felt in charge of her own destiny. That was it! If she left it up to Craig, she would be a doormat wife, being cheated on by her high-flying narcissistic husband. He'd gotten bored of her and had joined the cliché club by fucking the first teenager that would go for it. She felt embarrassed by the whole thing.

A little later that afternoon, she woke up in her sumptuous hotel bed, feeling completely rested and relaxed. She enjoyed the tropical shower that was in the en suite to wash the oils off her back. She took her time to wash her hair and as her skin was being cleaned, the euphoria began to wear off and she re-alised she was spending the night alone in a hotel room when she could go home and possibly catch her husband red-handed. *Surely he wouldn't take her to our house? She probably lives with her parents, so maybe he would?* Hannah's heart began to race as she thought this could be her chance to end the lies rather than prolonging the agony.

After what a had been such a thrilling ride, she decided that is was time to go home and face the mu-sic. She had no idea what she was going to walk into, but it could be life-changing.

14

ALICE

Alice kicked off her trainers and skipped up the stairs following her evening yoga class, feeling loose and light. Everything felt so good and she began experiencing gratitude for everything. Even little things, like how soft and fluffy the carpet felt beneath her feet. How lucky she was to be able to come home to a peaceful environment, no drama, no eggshells. This was her space and it was safe. It was clean. It was tidy and recently she had begun making it more homely and pretty.

There had been nights where she couldn't face another evening on her own. The loneliness was crippling. Now, she was fit and healthy and making good choices, she embraced her time, and felt safe in the knowledge that it was unlikely to last forever. She would tell herself to make the most of this free living. She didn't have to wait to use the shower. She didn't have to pick up anyone's socks. She got to have what she wanted for dinner every night and, one day, she would have to deal with all of the above on the flip side, and she smiled to herself at the idea of that. Until such day, she would enjoy the freedom knowing, and hoping, that one day she would have to learn to compromise again.

She stepped into the shower and let the tumbling beads of water pour down onto her head, reciting a mantra in her mind about washing away all that no longer served her. Allowing the water to cleanse her skin and take away any toxins and negative thoughts and feelings.

After her shower, she admired her body in her floor-to-ceiling bedroom mirror. When she had been doing a bottle of wine a night, she had a permanently bloated stomach. Even though she was slim, the stomach was always bloated. Now, she was toned and in great shape. She liked what she saw. She pulled on some skinny jeans that sculpted her thin and toned legs and threw on a loose blouse that hid her slight frame.

Twenty minutes later, she was in the local super-market looking at a selection of salmon fillets. In her basket: tender stem broccoli and a pouch of new pota-toes, the ones that could be steamed in the microwave in two minutes. She had had an internal battle about whether micro-steaming was actually that healthy but decided that the broccoli and salmon was good enough and micro-steamed potatoes was one less dish to wash up.

As she ran her fingers along the packets of fish on the shelf, she heard a voice she recognised, which caused the hairs on the back of her neck to stand. Suddenly, she felt very uneasy. She turned around slowly to look behind her and there he was. He was laughing and being very animated, and he was with a very attractive woman. Alice began to shake as her stomach started knotting. She looked at them. Her heart sank out of her body and beneath the ground. Then the woman saw her staring. Alice couldn't stand how pretty she was. Long flowing wavy hair. Tanned skin. Tall and skinny. She looked like she belonged on the cover of a magazine—the bohemian edition. Alice wanted to burst into tears and run.

The woman whispered something to him, and Dan turned around. Alice flinched. He looked her up and down like she was scum. Alice felt her chin begin to wobble. *Don't let him do this to you Alice. Walk away. Show him you don't care.*

Slowly, she turned around and began to walk away from them when she heard him say, 'No one important.' The lump escaped her throat and her eyes started to sting with the tears she was fighting. She abandoned her basket and made her way to the back of the store. To the alcohol aisle.

The following morning, Alice woke to her alarm shrieking in her ear. She pulled her pillow over her head and thumped the alarm into silence. Her mouth was almost dried shut and she could tell she was already in a foul mood. She rolled from side to side, keeping the pillow pulled over her head the whole time. She stretched out straight, then curled up, then straight again, before lying on her back, facing the ceiling, and throwing her pillow to the side. She rubbed her head and sighed, knowing that last night's weakness was going to ruin today and that she now faced a battle for the next eighteen hours. Alcohol was already on her mind. It was on her mind because she had stupidly crumbled the night before and now it was all she could think of was hair of the dog at lunchtime, followed by a few in the afternoon, and a comforting bottle of wine in the evening to see her through to bedtime. She rolled over and snatched her phone from the side.

'Oh God, no.' She looked in disbelief at the text from Dan, which read: 'Stop fucking phoning me, you psycho.' She launched it across the room and screamed in frustration. She got out of bed and started pacing her bedroom.

You've got two choices today Alice. You get a grip, go for a run, and deal with the horror for one day, and start afresh tomorrow ... or you can go to the offy, buy a bottle, curl up in front of the TV, and numb your mind from the pain you are living in. Jogging and dealing with things? Or drinking and not dealing with things?

She went downstairs and put on the coffee machine. She tapped her fingers frantically as the water began to steam. Images flashing into her mind of messages sent, phone calls made, anger, frustration, sadness ... *oh, the sadness.* She bit her lip anxiously. The thing that annoyed her the most was that she wasn't as sad as alcohol would have her believe. She had been so happy recently. The poison threw her way off the scale into a pit of irrationality. It wasn't her. It was as if she became possessed and a new version took over. This wasn't even a little bit of drunkenness. This was complete personality transformation. It was scary. She pulled the tray out of the coffee machine, dumped the old ones into the bin, and popped a new capsule in. *Don't let one slip ruin months of effort, Alice. Have a coffee, get in the shower, and go for a walk. You've got this. You are not that girl. Dan can think what he likes. Come on. You are better than this.*

Feeling empowered, Alice went up the stairs in a much better mood than she came down in. Today was going to be a good day. She was claiming it.

15

OLLIE

Ollie pulled the duvet closer, pulling it up across his face with only his wild hair sticking out. He wanted to block out the day that was pushing in through the curtains as he resisted his body waking up. He didn't want to be awake. Everything was manageable when he was asleep. He wasn't in pain when he was asleep. He wasn't looking for his mother when he was asleep. He didn't panic about what his future was going to be like when he was asleep.

He pulled his mobile up from the side of the bed and looked up his mum's Facebook page. A slight pang of guilt hit him about not having photos of her on his phone. They hadn't spent any quality time together in recent years. Mainly because, in his opinion, she was an idiot drunk and, according to her, he was an ungrateful teenager. How he regretted that now. She was a drunk, but he could've made more of an effort. Something that was never going to be an option ever again. He heard the murmurings of Sky and her mum in the kitchen and felt a sense of relief wash over him that at least he had them both. He wasn't alone. Even if it was just for now. They hadn't yet discussed where he would go, again something else that offered him a slight sense of solace. The murmuring stopped, and he heard the padding of footsteps coming up the stairs and heading towards his room. He swiped his hair back away from his face and removed the sleepy dust from his eyes.

There was a gentle tapping on the door, followed by Sky asking quietly if he was awake.

'Sure. Come in.' He gave half a smile.

Sky curled a smile back at him and put a steaming hot cup of tea on the bedside table next to him, noticing his skinny arms and pale complexion. 'I've put a spoon of sugar in it. Always makes me feel better when I am running on empty. Anyway, shall we find something to do today? I was thinking we should go for a walk, if you are up to it? Maybe even do some photography to take your mind off things?'

'Yeah, ok. Sounds good. To be honest, I just feel numb. I don't think it has really hit me yet. It's like they all say, it's as if she is just in another room. Perhaps I will feel different after the funeral. What is really strange is that I am sleeping really well, and I feel bad about that.'

Sky perched on the bed next to him and he got a waft of her scent. She smelled divine and he wished he could nuzzle into her neck and inhale deeply.

'Why do you feel bad about that? Your body is recouping from the grief. It's keeping you alive. You need the sleep right now.'

'I think I feel bad because this house is so peaceful. It's so calm. It's safe, you know? My house, I never knew if I was going to be woken up by something breaking, someone shouting, or my mum barging into my room at midnight, reeking of booze, and sitting on my bed telling me about when I was a baby.'

Sky edged forward and put her arms around Ollie, bringing his head onto her shoulder. She squeezed him tightly and he felt addicted to the affect she had on him. He didn't resist. He let his head rest in the soft crook of her curvaceous frame. She rocked him slightly and he thought if only he could stay like this forever. He realised that she was behaving like a big sister around him but if that was all that was on offer, he would take it. He was falling for her but would never have the confidence to do anything about it anyway, so she didn't need to know. He would just follow her lead. If she came close, he would allow it, but he would never pre-empt anything. He was already terrified of losing her, the bits of her she gave to him. As long as he had her, he could make it through this. He breathed in again and enjoyed the coconut scent from her thick afro braids that were draping across his face.

'Well, drink your tea, and then we can head out. Mum said she can drop us off somewhere if you fancy a change of scene. What do you fancy photographing? Sea, woods, or city?

'How about we go to the old castle ruins in Netley, and then we could always walk along the shore after, if we fancy? Have some chips on the beach perhaps? I need to phone my grandmother and see if she needs my help with anything. She was very matter-of-fact when I spoke to her the other day. I know they hadn't spoken for years, but I did expect her to be a little bit upset. If anything, she sounded annoyed and said that she would do all the necessary "admin".'

'She probably *is* annoyed. She saw her daughter waste her life and now she has left her son. She is probably really disappointed in her and feels bad for you. Let her do the "admin"; it's her way of helping you, I think. Taking away one less strain, or probably many strains. She'll have bank accounts to close down, utilities to sort out, funeral arrangements. There will be loads to do. I think calling her again is a good idea, maybe try and build a relationship. You might find that you two can have a fulfilling relationship now your mother has gone. It sounded to me like you missed out on having your grandparents around because of their own frustrations with her. Anyway, get dressed and let's go out.'

Sky stood by the bedroom door and smiled at him. He loved everything about her. Even the lilac eyeshadow that she was wearing today, which was a bit out there. He couldn't imagine a time when she could ever look bad. She smiled, his heart fluttered, and she left him to get ready.

Hannah had been urging her period to stay away but unfortunately it was not meant to be. Two weeks after her dangerous liaison it arrived bang on time. She had been frantically searching for early pregnancy symptoms. Lower back ache. Sore breasts. Fatigue. Moodiness. 'Great,' she thought. 'So, basically all the symptoms of a period coming.'

She had been having smoothies for breakfast, jacket potatoes or soup for lunch, and chicken or salmon for dinner. She had gone swimming three times a week and had not touched any alcohol. She had done everything in her power to help that egg get fertilized.

Craig hadn't noticed. He had barely been at home and Hannah tried her very best to not think about where he could be or who with. The thought that a tiny little person might be growing inside her was enough to keep her happy for now. Once she knew for sure that she was pregnant, she would tell Craig and he would realise that his silly little affair needed to end and that he loved her and that they would finally have the family they had both longed for so much.

When the day came, and she noticed the pink on the tissue after wiping, her heart sank. She screamed. She threw her phone across the room. She sobbed. She was losing her husband and she was losing her chance of being a mother. That day she opened the gin and lay on the sofa all afternoon.

Craig came back that evening. 'Knew it wouldn't last long,' he said, looking at the bottle and the glass next to her. He stood there in his tennis kit with a towel draped around his shoulders, his thick wet hair flopping around his face.

Hannah leapt up from the sofa. Her feelings of heartbreak and deceit mounting in her head like an avalanche. 'Fuck you, Craig. Fuck you and fuck that teenager you are fucking too.' Hannah's big blues eyes filled up with tears, her usually pale complexion now a very visible crimson. The pain in her face equally visible.

Craig looked crestfallen and froze to the spot as he saw his wife's tear-stained face look at him, the pain visible, the heartbreak undeniable. She ran out to the hallway, grabbed her bag, and slammed the door as she left in a whirlwind.

'Shit,' was all he could say as he slowly sat on the arm of the sofa and watched the door slam shut.

Craig put his head in his hands. Suddenly, the reality of his actions sank in. He never wanted to hurt Hannah. He loved her. Things had been tough, and he had been weak. Right now, all he wanted was Hannah back and to tell her he would end it immediately. His mind was flooding with thoughts. *How did she know? Did she find out today, or had she known prior to today?*

Suddenly, he felt like an absolute jerk. The look

he saw on her face as she left had him feeling like a piece of shit. No matter how bad things were, she would never do to him what he had done to her. He knew she loved him. He knew she was not going anywhere, and he had betrayed her and she knew it was with a younger woman. She didn't deserve it. He should've just told her he wasn't happy and that they needed some time apart. He felt pathetic for needing to have sex elsewhere to make him feel good about himself.

That being said, she was so needy. He had felt trapped and Hayley had just been there at the right time. All he and Hannah did was argue these days. She had become obsessed with having a baby and after months and months of watching her get her hopes up and then watching them be dashed, he didn't know how to tell her he was infertile. After months of trying and Hannah becoming obsessed with a baby and nothing else, they both got tested. They had already grown apart by this point. She had made sex so conception-orientated that he had lost interest. She had become crabby and looking back, they had both started to grow apart. She got her results back. Fine. He got his. Not good. He had nothing. It was very unlikely that he would ever have a child with his own sperm. In a moment of disbelief and panic, he told her he was fine, but with a slightly low sperm count and that the advice he was given was that they should both relax a little and it would work for them in good time.

Each month, when Hannah got her period, she would lash out at him as if it was his fault, which he resented. Deep down, he knew her grief was his fault. He had lied to her about his sperm and she was getting her hopes up every month and he knew he could've prevented that. He wasn't sure why he'd lied to her. Well, that wasn't strictly true. Around the time he got his results, Hayley had started flirting with him at the tennis club. Finding out he couldn't have children had made him feel less of a man. An attractive twenty-one year-old made him feel much more of a man.

He didn't hesitate to go for it when he knew for certain she was game. She had pretty much thrown herself at him. He had been in the changing room getting dressed. The club was closing and he was the last one in there, deliberately on his part. She had knocked on the door and said she needed to check the lockers. She walked right towards him and dropped something just past his feet. Then, right there in front of him, she slowly bent down to pick it up revealing a G-string under her tennis skirt. His shorts were about to explode. She looked over her shoulder and looked up at him and saw his erection sticking out—and right there and then she pulled her t-shirt over her head.

He grabbed her and began kissing her passionately. He pinned her against the lockers with his body and she spread her legs for him. In no time at all, he had pulled his shorts down. He was throbbing and eager and shoved himself hard between her legs. He almost came there and then. He picked her up and she wrapped her legs around him. She moaned loudly and he thrust hard. He only managed three thrusts and it was over. He slammed her against the lockers and she kept herself wrapped around him.

'Well, that was naughty,' she whispered before gently landing her feet back on the floor. She pulled her G-string back in place and winked at him. 'See you soon.'

And just like that she was gone again. He could hardly believe that had actually happened. It was like a dream. A fantasy played out in real life. He shook his head, pulled up his shorts, and got his stuff and left. That was how the affair began. It was just sex at first. Usually at the club after tennis. They had sex several times and then he began buying her presents to keep her sweet. He thought back to the time he took her to the new French restaurant that Hannah had wanted to go to and felt another pang of guilt. He didn't want Hayley. She was fun and sexy, but they had nothing in common. He had betrayed his wife and now feared he was going to lose everything.

PHIL

Phil was looking at Alice's Facebook profile with one hand down his pants. He particularly enjoyed her photo album of her on holiday in Croatia. She was with her boyfriend and there were lots of bikini shots in there. Just enough resource and his imagination could do the rest. He didn't need much. He hadn't had sex in so long that a few quick tugs looking at her photos, imagining what the rest looked like and he was done. As soon as he had, he slammed closed his laptop and pulled his boxers back on without cleaning up first. With a smile on his face he walked through his grotty little flat and lit up a cigarette, leaning out of the living room window and scratching his back side. His starved collie mongrel came over and started sniffing around his crotch. Phil looked at the dog and took another drag of his cigarette. He flicked it out of the window and closed the curtains. Looking at the dog again, Phil's mind began to wander to a dark place. He looked at the dog. The dog tilted its head, it's big marble like eyes pleading for some food. Phil played with the elastic waistband of his jogging bottoms. Then he had an idea. He walked into the kitchen and got a tin of dog food. He peeled back the foil lid and carried it through to the living room.

'Dinner time.' He laughed.

The dog was starving and began to whine and lick around his mouth. He opened the tin of food and looked down at his crotch as he chewed on his bottom lip. *Come on Phil. You are not that desperate and that idea is definitely illegal. Don't do it.* He hesitated as he battled with his own thoughts. He just wanted to be touched so badly and he wondered if he revealed himself, would the dog still try and sniff his crotch. Suddenly he snapped out of the dark place he had ventured to in his mind. He shoved the dog away and laid back on the sofa feeling unsettled. He was desperate for sex and getting bored of watching porn or looking at old magazines.

Ever since he got sacked form the local secondary school, no woman had gone near him. Although Lindsay Palmer's accusations were never proved, the rumours circulated like wildfire and life had never been the same again. He had been taunted in the street. Names hurled at him. *Paedo. Sick bastard.* You name it, he had been called it. He had even got jumped one evening by a group of young lads. They didn't give him much of a kick in. They just roughed him up a bit and called him some names. Eventually, the gossip died down. Sometimes people would still cross the street to the other side if they walked near him but for the most part, life had moved on. The good thing about his pub that he had, was that most of the people that drank in there regularly had problems of their own. They didn't seem to judge him. They were there to numb their own pain.

Phil made his way to the shower and had a slight

spring in his step following his morning relief. He stepped into his mould ridden shower cubicle of which the tray was lined with scum. He whistled as he washed his overweight body, ideas of having sex with anyone that would have him racing through his perverted mind. He gave his willy a shake and began laughing. *Life was not too bad*, he thought to himself. He loved running his pub, he loved not having the responsibility of being a school teacher now. He could do what he liked, and no one cared. He could have breakfast beer and that put a smile on his face.

He stepped out of the shower and picked up his dirty old towel which was only just big enough to be wrapped round his waist. He combed back his thinning hair in his toothpaste flecked mirror, winking at himself like the champ that he thought he was. He slapped some cheap aftershave on his face and rubbed it in and onto his neck and chest.

Once he was dressed, he sat on the edge of his bed and tentatively opened up his bedside drawer. He paused for a moment to look around him knowing that no one could see but felt he needed to check anyway. He picked up the small, clear snap bag and opened it whilst taking a sniff under his nose. He sprinkled a small pile of white powder onto his fist and snorted it in one go, knocking his head back as he did so and shuddering afterwards. He pinched his nose to stem the burning sensation and winced as it dropped down the back of his throat. He stood up and rumbled on his chest and set about clearing the pig sty that he lived in.

18

ALICE

Alice looked in the mirror and tidied the scarf wrapped loosely around her neck. She gave herself an approving nod and a slightly smug smile. 'It's not smug. You are taking back your power,' she thought to herself.

After she had gotten out of the shower that morning, her best friend Sarah had sent her a text asking if she was free for a coffee. It was just what she needed. She was avoiding the crippling booze cravings but also didn't need to punish herself with a painful 5K run. A sophisticated coffee and a catch-up with a good friend was the perfect antidote. Alice knew she had a very bad habit (another one) of bunkering down when things were tough. It wasn't as if she were hiding. She wasn't more sad than normal or in a dark place; it was some kind of self-preservation mode. It also wasn't a conscious thing; she didn't set out to hide. It was as if her battery was on ten percent and she needed to lie low until it was back up to fifty. It didn't enter her mind to reach out to people. She had to stay away from people to recharge. It also didn't faze her that her friends didn't check on her; when she was like this she didn't want to be checked on. It was not until she was having an up day, and then she might question why she was the one to always reach out. She had been bunkering down for the last few weeks and seeing Sarah today was a welcome and much needed surprise.

Sarah and Alice were childhood friends. Their mums had met when they were pregnant and became close friends, and so the girls were almost brought up like sisters, or cousins perhaps. As with all friendships, sometimes the women were closer and sometimes they did not see each other for a while. The same had happened with Alice and Sarah. Alice would see more of Sarah when she was single. Alice didn't mind that for the most part because she felt Sarah was more authentic during these times. When Sarah did meet a guy, it seemed to Alice as though Sarah always rushed things and was desperate to make it serious. She also became someone she wasn't really, which of course never lasted. The cracks would show, and the guys would leave because of her temper. Her temper being her own frustration that she wasn't getting her own way, despite adopting all of their interests and changing her likes and dislikes to match theirs. The guy of the moment had fallen for the newly coupled Sarah, not the 'move in with me now' Sarah. Sarah would then flee to Alice's with a bottle of wine, sobbing for the evening whilst telling Alice what a wanker Dan was and how she could do better. Alice also thought Sarah could do better for herself if she just let things play out for themselves sometimes, and to stop putting so much pressure on things.

Alice didn't know what today's meet-up was

about. Sarah had been seeing Lewis for a while now. She only occasionally asked Sarah if she was free these days because it would take Sarah several days to reply, and as much as this made Alice feel sad, she didn't want to completely kibosh the friendship. Sarah was either about to tell her she was moving in with Lewis, she had broken up with Lewis, or just wanted to have a coffee and pretend to be interested in Alice's news. Alice really didn't mind either today. She just needed to get out of the house, ignore the 'hangxiety', block out the booze shame, and move on with the day. Sarah was exactly what she needed today.

She put on a slick of peach lipstick, pouted her lips, and said, 'Ignore the critics that live in your head, Alice. You're not as bad as they would have you believe.' One more final glance in the mirror, she pulled on her mittens, and she was good to go—at least as good as she could be.

As she pulled the key out of the lock and put it in her bag, the screen of her mobile lit up. It was Dan. She froze as a wave of panic ran over her. *Be strong, Alice. He is not good for your mental health.*

'Shall we talk later today?'

She examined the text and read it over and over again, chewing at her lip as she did so. *Maybe he wants me back.* She began to feel happy about that but was reminded by a voice inside her head that said, 'Think about how you feel *after* you have seen him. It does not end well. You are far stronger without him. Don't let him rip you to shreds again.'

Alice felt her stomach smile and she whipped off her mittens and picked up her phone and typed, 'No.' She tossed the mobile back into her bag and set off in the crisp Spring air to meet her friend, determined that one bump in the road did not define her.

As Alice approached Sarah by the cenotaph, she noticed immediately that Sarah was picking her fingernails; she was shuffling nervously on the spot and making eye contact one minute with an awkward smile and then looking away the next. 'This looks interesting,' Alice thought as she edged closer to Sarah, offering a friendly embrace.

'Alice! Look at you. Have you been working out? You look fab!' exclaimed Sarah, still carrying an air of nervousness about her.

'Are you cracking on to me?' laughed Alice. 'You look fab today and this was a very welcome surprise. It's good to see a friendly face.' She gave her a loose hug.

'Is it! it is.' Sarah latched on to Alice and squeezed her hard. 'It's always good to see friends and remember that friends are always friends, and nothing changes that. Friends are better than family in fact.'

Alice stepped back and looked at Sarah with a furrowed brow.

'Ah-hh.' The cold air escaped Sarah's mouth and formed a cloud of Spring freshness around them. Placing her hand on Alice's shoulder, Sarah said, 'Let's walk. Coffee? This way. There must be something down here.'

Alice followed Sarah's lead with tentative steps as the saliva built up her mouth.

'What's going on, Sarah? I'm sensing you need to tell me something.'

They continued to walk down Southampton High Street, past Guildhall Square, Alice noting that Sarah was avoiding eye contact at all costs and was acting shiftier than she had ever seen before. A knot the size of the rubber band ball she'd made in primary six was forming in her stomach.

'Oh, I've got loads to tell you actually. Loads. Some good, but let's catch up first. Let's not spoil the morning. In fact, it's nearly lunchtime. Fancy a toastie?'

'Well, actually, Sarah … suddenly, I'm not very hungry. What's going on? Are you ok? Are you sick?' Alice stopped, and it took Sarah a few more steps before she noticed.

'No, no. It's not me. I'm fine. Come on. Let's get coffee or maybe tea. Tea is more soothing.'

Alice shrugged in frustration and followed her friend towards the coffee shop.

The pair found a table in the corner of a bustling, noisy café. Chairs scraping across floors, coffee machines screaming into life. The cacophony of general chatter. Windows steamed with condensation and the little pockets of traffic noise each time the door opened and closed. They took it in turns to offer snippets of conversation. Occasionally asking the other to repeat themselves due to the clinking of cups and the sound of the bell reverberating each time the door opened. If you looked in through the window, it was a pleasant site. Two girls, coats on backs of seats, bags discarded by their feet, both leaning in with elbows on the table, taking it in turns to laugh; all the while, if you looked at their feet under the table, you would see that each was as nervous as the other as they constantly tapped a foot or crossed their legs, and then switched over. The windows getting increasingly steamed up as the lunchtime rush took place.

Sarah came back from the loo, the loud screeching

of her chair on the tiled floor breaking up the day-dream that Alice was in. 'Ok. I'll put you out of your misery. There are two things. I'll start with the first, less serious one. Lewis has asked me to marry him.'

Alice's eyes darted to a bare ring finger. 'And this is the less serious topic? You have said no?' Eyes again looking at the finger and back at Sarah. 'This is what you have been dreaming of. You have literally been talking about this since you met ... two ... three years ago.'

'Two years and four months. I don't know Alice. I do want it, I want it so much, I just don't know if it's with Lewis. There's this guy ...'

'Oh, hell no. Don't even. Lewis adores you. What the hell are you thinking?'

'Stop. I hate myself more than you can know. Nothing has happened. That's the first thing. The second thing is we both want it to, but I am also scared this might be the only proposal I get, and I am not getting any younger.'

'Oh my God, Sarah. You are literally the last person I ever thought I would have this conversation with.'

'I know. It's shit, isn't it?' Sarah looked into her coffee like a child asking to be forgiven for being naughty.

'Sarah, this is serious. I am not going to give you the greenlight on this. I am going to help you reach a decision, but I will not let you do what I think it is that you want. God.' Alice sat back and brushed her hair away from her face before leaning back in. 'It's me that is the fuck-up, not you. I can't sit back and let you do this. I am the one that ruins everything. You are the one who saves for a mortgage and bakes cakes on the weekend. Please don't fuck this up. Tell me everything from the start. Go.'

Sarah sipped carefully from her hot mug of coffee before putting it down slower than was necessary.

'I don't know where to start. I don't remember where the beginning is ... was. I am trying to make sense of it all. The more I look back, the more I think I was putting Lewis into a box he didn't belong in. Basically, he loves me. I know that. He loves me more than I love him, I know that too, but that was deliberate on my part. I've always been too scared to love someone fully. Having someone who is not a risk makes me feel safe. I know he's not going anywhere. I know he would never cheat on me. That is part of the appeal. Don't get me wrong. I love him, but I know I will never love him as much as he loves me.' Sarah exhaled loudly and looked deep in thought. She picked up a blueberry muffin and stuffed half into her mouth in one bite as Alice looked on, wondering how she could even eat right now. The slightest bit of stress in her life shut down her hunger immediately. 'Mmm, that's a bloody good muffin. Anyway, where was I?'

'The bit where he loves you more,' Alice replied in disbelief.

'Oh yeah. So, I know that sounds bad, but it's actually not. If I was with someone and loved them more, I'd be permanently insecure and that would make me hard work as a girlfriend, not to mention how miserable I would feel at the prospect of having the love of my life snatched away from me by anyone. I just can't live like that. Plus, I read in a magazine that someone always loves the other one more in a relationship. I am happy for that someone not to be me.'

'How very noble of you,' Alice said, pulling at her bra strap, feeling uncomfortable and itchy.

'That's not very ladylike, you know. You shouldn't play with your bra strap like that; you'll put men off.'

Alice stopped in her tracks and locked eyes with Sarah.

'I'm only trying to help. Anyway, the whole Lewis thing. Now that I have got what I wanted, I'm just wondering if there is more to life.'

'No, you're not. You're thinking about shagging this other guy.'

Sarah spluttered on her coffee.

'What? I'm only telling the truth. So, let's get to how he came about.' Alice looked at Sarah as if she had just returned from a late night of drinking vodka in a field as a teenager trying desperately to turn the key in the lock as quietly as she could, only to find Alice standing on the other side of the door.

'He's a guy at work. He started a few months ago. Nothing has happened ... well, I say nothing. One thing has happened and that's why I need to call off the wedding.'

Alice stayed silent and continued to drink her coffee, willing Sarah to continue. 'One night ... after work ... basically, my bottom drawer at work was stuck and it had my train ticket in it, and I couldn't get it to open.'

Alice shuffled in her seat and crossed her legs the other way whilst keeping her eyes fixed on Sarah. Sarah went to speak but stopped herself. She took a mouthful of coffee and put the cup back. 'Oh, come on for fuck's sake, just tell me,' pleaded Alice.

'I went home and basically, I'—pausing, she

looked around before continuing—'pleasured myself as I thought about him.'

Two men about ten years older than them paused as they passed the table holding their cardboard take-away cups and gave Sarah a kinky smile. Sarah's face flushed with a medley of crimson shades. Alice burst out laughing. Her head rolled back, her chest heaving up and down, her hand slapping her knee. She howled as Sarah begged her to be quiet.

'Will you shut up? It is *not* funny. This is my life,' said Sarah in frustration.

'Is that it?' she asked, wiping a tear away with her wrist.

'Shut up,' begged Sarah and exclaimed, 'Shut up *now*!'

'Sarah, masturbating is perfectly normal. It's not cheating.' Alice noticed Sarah flinch in disgust and continued laughing, her shoulders going up and down with each hearty chortle. 'In fact, I would say this is perfectly healthy. It all points towards cold feet and nerves. Go home, make love to your fiancé. Every-thing is fine. It's ok to find someone else attractive. You love Lewis. You might be scared to admit it, but you do. You're perfect for each other. Now, what was the other thing you wanted to talk to me about?'

Sarah bit her lip. Alice's brow furrowed and she sat up straight, noticing the atmosphere had become very tense.

'Alice, this is really difficult.'

Alice picked up her coffee mug and held it to her mouth, waiting nervously for further information.

'Actually, let me ask you this. How are things with Dan?'

Alice inhaled deeply and looked out the window

at the passers-by. She half turned her body away from Sarah and crossed her legs. She pulled the sleeves of her top over her hands and clenched the fabric in her fists. 'I guess you could say not great. I was doing really well. I gave up drinking and was feeling a lot happier about things, but then I saw him yesterday in the shop, and he was with some girl. He dismissed me as if I was nothing. He told her I was no one. How can I be a nobody? We had three years together.' She looked back out of the window.

'Who was the girl?'

'I don't know but she was gorgeous. I assumed it was someone he is seeing.'

'He is such a cock. This makes this even worse.'

'Makes what worse?' Alice shifted in her seat and faced Sarah. Her top was no longer clenched in her fists.

'Alice, I'm sorry. It's just that ... well ... my sister. Rachel. She's seeing Dan.'

Alice's jaw dropped. Her eyes darkened a shade. She looked at the floor, then back up at Sarah. 'Rachel? And Dan? Dan and Rachel together? But Rachel knows he is ... was my Dan.' Alice stared at Sarah, her face crinkled with confusion.

'I know, and I have tried speaking to her, but Rachel doesn't care about other people. She gets whatever she wants. She basically said you guys ended ages ago and it's a free country. I'm sorry about my younger sister, but I wanted you to hear it from me. '

Alice hunched over, as if in physical pain. She had gone back to staring out of the window, knees bent in together, feet facing inward.

Sarah noticed how vulnerable she looked. The

way she was sitting was like she was cowering in a corner. Sarah began to feel bad that she hadn't been there for Alice during the break-up. She was noticing that it had been harder on Alice than she had realised. 'Shall we go for a drink, would that help? I can spend the day with you. I don't have anywhere to be, so let's go and take your mind off it.'

Alice said nothing. Sarah wasn't sure if Alice had even heard her, but she did see that her chin was wobbling. 'It was going to happen at some point. You *will* be ok. I'm here for you. It hurts right now, but something better is out there for you. Anyway, tell me more about the girl he was with yesterday.'

19

OLLIE

As Sky's mother waved goodbye to them both, Ollie was watching them smiling at each other and admiring how beautiful they both were. The big beaming smiles, the dense hair, the perfect skin, and their waif-like arms waving back and forth gently, as if in motion with the wind. As Ollie averted his gaze and attempted feebly to wave back at Gwen, Sky's mother, she paused and curled her smile inwards. She had seen him staring at Sky and she felt sorry that he had no one, he told himself. He returned a smile and sheepishly looked away. She was almost too beautiful to look at too.

Sky hoisted her backpack onto her shoulder and sighed at its heaviness.

'Right then. Let's go to Netley Abbey ... or we could go to Royal Victoria Country Park. Ooh! We could walk up to the military graveyard and get some cool shots up there, if you like. I don't mind, it's your day, Ollie Wollie.' She ruffled his hair, which he didn't mind but noted it wasn't something she had done before. It seemed to him as though she were putting a barrier between them by belittling him that way.

'Yeah cool, let's do that,' he said, trying to ignore what the hair ruffle had been about.

Sky marched on ahead with long strides, chewing gum, and looking as cool as ever, Ollie thought. He loved her style. Her attitude. Her attitude was unspoken, but it was very clearly there. She turned around to see where he was, and with his camera poised, he captured her in the perfect shot. She was wearing Doc Martins with pop socks and denim hot pants. Her top half was a purple tank top that covered her svelte but womanly frame and hugged her toned torso. Her afro was scooped up on top of her head. She wore sixties style circular sunglasses and large hoop earrings.

As she had turned to look back at him, she held the backpack loosely by the straps and stood there as if she had one stinking attitude, whilst chewing her gum animatedly.

'Incredible. You're a natural, Sky. Simply stunning!' He could tell she had rolled her eyes behind those dark lenses.

Ollie snapped away, taking pictures of the duck pond on the left and then the shore on the right. Sky turning occasionally to check he was still behind her. He noticed each turn and ran to catch her up, his hand skimming hers as he met her. She didn't flinch or move away from him. In fact, she bumped into him quite a lot when they walked side by side. As they walked up the road towards the main park, Sky asked him what he wanted to talk about, encouraging him subtly to talk about his mum, knowing that he did not want to.

Ollie had said he didn't have much to say for himself and instead asked her to tell him something about her life. Anything, a chapter he didn't know about yet. Sky chewed faster as she thought about something that was interesting to tell him. 'I could tell you about my first kiss, if you like. The first time someone tried to bully me. The times when I have felt scared. The stupidest thing I have done. What do you want to know?'

'I can't see you doing anything stupid. You always seem so determined and confident.'

'There lieth the problem,' she said with an animated wink.

Ollie thought about her first kiss. He thought about her lips on his and felt his trousers getting tighter around his groin. Panicking, he forced other images into his mind to calm himself. He saw her kissing another and quickly his trousers loosened up again.

'Hello? Hello? I lost you there. Where did you go?' asked Sky, examining Ollie's vacuous look.

'Nowhere really. Just thinking about stuff,' he replied, looking at his shoes.

'Right, come on. What you need are some natural endorphins. Race you to the third lamppost.' Before he could count the lampposts ahead of him, Sky was off. He hung his camera round his neck and began a feeble attempt at catching her up, enjoying the view in front of him.

'Loser buys the chips later,' she called behind her.

'I'll buy you anything you want,' whispered Ollie. He finally made it to the lamppost that she was casually leaning against, laughing at how out of breath he was.

'Feels good, doesn't it? If you feel low, you need to move. Works for me.'

'Can't say I'm with you on that one. Not yet,' he said, trying to catch his breath and trying not to be seen looking at her breasts, jiggling as she laughed in front of him.

They walked across the vast field of the old military hospital grounds. Sky had that natural 'gratitude attitude' and had a thirst for life. He wished he had an ounce of her energy.

'Do you want to know a cool fact about that building?' He pointed at the museum.

'Always,' said Sky.

'Look at the windows. Look how big they are. This building and another were designed by the same architect. One was for here and the other was meant for somewhere in India. The schematics got mixed up and this is the one that should have been built in India; hence, the massive windows for the heat. So, somewhere in India, is a hospital meant for the UK and with much smaller windows.'

'Is that right? Wow. That is a cool fact. I love it. How do you know so much stuff?' Sky asked with genuine wonderment.

'Spent a lot of time alone, reading.'

Sky put an arm around his shoulders, and they walked together towards the graveyard; she was slightly taller than him in her platform boots, and he didn't mind at all.

Once they arrived at the graveyard, Ollie was in his element. Lying on the damp grass taking snaps, climbing up into trees, balancing on the old rickety branches.

'Strange isn't it ... so much courage and sadness in

one place. So much bravery, yet so much defeat. Some of these were just young boys. Men, fathers, brothers. All brothers in the end. We just can't even imagine what it must've been like.'

'Strangers we came together ... as brothers we depart ... all to lie together in the end and to sleep under the stars.'

Ollie was hanging off every word Sky said, watching her compassion for others spill out of her mouth. Gratitude even for those she'd never met but understood their sacrifice.

'That's beautiful. You should write it down.'

Sky stood and stared at the graves and slowly came out of the trance she seemed to be in. 'I'm not the creative one. That's you,' she said as she walked around, kicking the leaves beneath her. 'Ollie, I know you don't want to talk about her, but she was still your mum, and the more I think about it, the more I think you have to believe she loved you. Alcohol didn't define her. Yes, she got caught in a trap, but she was always there. I've got a feeling she's up there now, looking down on you as the only thing she got right, wishing she could have her chance with you again but also feeling glad that she couldn't let you down anymore.

'When I think about parents, yes, I'm lucky with my mum, but it's a huge risk having a baby. How can anyone know they are going to be any good at it? It's got to be the biggest pressure in the world. To protect another forever and love them and provide for them and help them to learn and be fun and be strict. It's a lot. Maybe she didn't feel good enough for you, and drinking was the only way to feel less shit about herself.'

Ollie gazed ahead, Sky sitting next to him on the bench, trying ever so hard to not let that wobbling chin crumble completely. 'I feel so alone, Sky. So, fucking alone. I can't think about what's ahead for me because if I do, I see nothing. I just have to live each day.'

The tears began to pour and Sky pulled him in. She held Ollie as he sobbed, and she was grateful that they were in a quiet graveyard that no one else seemed to be interested in. The sun was beginning to set.

Ollie sobbed, his shoulders rising high and falling heavily with each outpour of grief. He needed it. This was progress in Sky's mind. She had actually become concerned that he wasn't showing any emotion and had hoped he was bottling it up. She was relieved that he was now allowing his grief to exit his body.

His crying began to slow down. The heavy breathing and gasps for breath were less. His body gradually moved towards stillness. Then he stopped. He was still. The crying was done. He brought his dirty cuff up to his face and swiped it across his nose and under his eyes.

Sky felt it was safe to let go of him and also thought his jacket must've felt rough on his face and got him a packet of tissues out of her backpack.

He stood up and looked around him. His black hair falling across his eyes. His skin flushed and a tear rolled down his cheek.

'Stay there,' said Sky. 'Don't move.' She grabbed his Nikon and told him to look to his left. She captured a photo of him and his single tear. 'Here you go. Call that one grief. It's real. It's raw.'

Ollie looked at the picture. He couldn't ignore the

fact that he didn't like looking at himself, but on this occasion, the picture was awesome. The wintery shade of sky, the bare branches of trees in a deserted graveyard. It was the perfect picture to call 'grief', as she had suggested. His flushed skin against the sun setting, the single tear ... it was an incredible photo. *Just a shame it's so real.*

'I'm so proud of you, Ollie. I don't mean that in a cheesy way. You are handling this better than you think, and look, I know I won the race earlier, but I'll get the chips. Come on, let's walk back to Netley. It's getting a bit cold actually. Fancy a couple of drinks to warm us up? Maybe a bottle of voddie?'

'Yeah. Sure. Sounds great, actually.'

The two picked up their things and walked off together as the sun was going down, leaving the grave-yard and tears behind them. Ollie threw his backpack over his shoulder and skimmed Sky's fingertips as he did so, and was pretty certain she touched his back, even if just a tiny bit. She definitely didn't flinch, he knew that much.

20

HANNAH, PHIL & ALICE

The evening was cold. It was dark and dewy outside, but Hannah knew this landscape well. They had lived in their house for six years and she had walked their dog up and down this road for the last two years. The dog that was to replace the baby that never came.

She marched furiously along, trying not to slip into the deep verge on the side. There were no street-lamps. It was a suburban lane in Hamble, with only five houses on it. All detached. All with grand gardens. All owned by wealthy families. *Homes built for families. Not for lonely, neglected housewives.* Even seeing the top of a trampoline sticking out above a fence would cause a pang of hurt. They had moved here to make room for a family and that hadn't happened. No baby and now her husband was cheating on her.

So many people would drive down a lane like this thinking the people that lived here must have it made. They had no idea about the hurt on the other side. What was the point of success if you couldn't have it all? Surely ambitious people wanted it all?

How does Craig feel about not having it all? Or

perhaps the baby stuff is not as important to him. He obviously needs more sex, more flattery, more adoration. She cursed as she continued walking determinedly along the lane, the sound of the busier roads creeping in and the streetlights appearing in the distance. *Maybe having it all was the wife and the mistress. Is she the first? Have there been others? Has our whole relationship been a lie?* Hannah stood and put her head in her hands. The anger was consuming her. The questions were coming in thick and fast, and all she could think was that she wasn't upset, she was angry. She had skipped the hurt stage.

Maybe I didn't love him either. Of course, I do. But he has been mistreating me for so long and now this. He has someone else and he doesn't care about me anymore. She reached the end of the lane and the twinkling lights of The Red Lion were in the distance. Gilbert's Brasserie was closer but too many people knew her in there. She needed to be left alone and go somewhere not really her scene. The Red Lion looked less friendly, or less obnoxious some might say. It was perfect for now. She needed a drink and some time alone to think things over.

A car honked as she recklessly ran across the road. She didn't apologise with a wave. If anything, she was disappointed they had slowed down. *Being dead would be less painful right now; I wish they had mown me down.* The dark thoughts passed through her head fleetingly. Standing outside the entrance to The Red Lion, she began to have second thoughts. There was a group of men blocking the doorway, smoking, talking and coughing loudly. Beneath the windows were neglected flowerbeds that probably didn't look any better in

Summer that they did now, she thought. Empty pint glasses here and there from boozers who'd had their last fag and left. She thought about turning back, but remembering Craig was her only other option encouraged her to squeeze past the men and make her way inside.

The difference with pubs like this was no one cared when you walked in. Not one person looked round. No one flinched. No one was sizing you up to see if you fit in. There was no code in a place like this. You could be anyone and no one cared. Suddenly, she felt calm for the first time that day.

An unkempt man, overweight and smelly, peeled himself off a bar stool and made his way behind the bar. 'What can I get you?' he asked whilst giving a very obvious stare to her chest before returning to her face with a smirk.

'Ah, um, I'll just have a large Sauvignon Blanc, please. New Zealand.' She smiled nervously.

Phil noticed the smudged mascara and the bloodshot eyes and laughed to himself. He looked in the fridge behind him, revealing a good amount of arse crack as he examined the labels. 'Australian ... that will do,' he whispered. He poured it into a glass with his back to her, so she couldn't see, and turned the bottle away as he presented it to her. 'Try it.' He smiled.

She took a sip sheepishly. 'Mmm, lovely. Thank you.'

Stupid stuck-up cow he thought as he put the bottle away and through the till rang through a large Malborough, New Zealand, which was more expensive than the Australian one he had given her.

"Aven't seen you in 'ere before. You local? I'm

Phil. I'm the landlord.' He thumped his fists on his chest as if he was a Flintstone.

Hannah took another sip as she noticed his grease-stained t-shirt and his dirty fingernails. She wasn't thinking about Craig any longer. She was thinking about how disgusting this venue and its owner was. She chuckled to herself.

'What? What's so funny?'

'I just needed to take my mind off something and this place has worked. That's all. I'm local-ish. My ... my husband and I ... we have a place down by the water.'

'Ooh, very nice. Don't know what brought you in here then. People who live by the water don't usually come in my pub. You'll find no airs and graces in 'ere. They're not welcome. Good food, tele, and beer. That's what this place is about.'

'It is just what I needed. A change of scene and I have heard about the food. Is it Steve? Local lad? He is a good cook, apparently.'

'Steve certainly is a good cook, but he has been taught well. By me.'

'Oh. I see. Are you a cook as well then?'

'No, but I am the leadership of this establishment.'

They both swapped confused glances and looked away. Hannah picked up her wine glass and nodded at Phil as she went to sit in a corner, ignoring his eyes as they went from her head to toes to head again.

Sarah barged in through the group of men that made various noises such as 'oi oi' and 'wahey' as she did so. She acknowledged them and pretended not to enjoy the attention as Alice shuffled in after her, oblivious to it all.

Phil managed to avert his gaze from Hannah when the two girls caught his eye, causing him to light up like a child in a Santa's Grotto.

'Fuck me, must be my lucky night,' he whispered under his breath, having never seen so many women in his pub before. He leapt off his bar stool and darted behind the bar and wiped his nose with the back of his hand.

'Lovely ladies, very lovely ladies. What can I get you? First one is on me. She looks like she needs it,' he said, gesturing at Alice who was gazing into the distance as if she had been given a sedative.

'Thanks, that's very kind of you,' Sarah said as she flicked her hair over her shoulder and checked her look in the mirror behind the bar.

'That's the kind of guy I am. Tell you what, any time you lovely ladies want to come into my pub, the first one is always on me.'

Sarah flickered her eyes and gave a coy smile.

'You seem like a lot of fun. What's wrong with your mate?'

'Boy trouble. What else?'

'Ah, we are a bad breed. Some right wankers out there, but we are not all like it. And not all the good ones are taken.' Phil winked and Sarah felt herself recoil as she looked at his beer belly stretching his grease-stained t -shirt.

Phil retrieved a bottle of house white out of the fridge and filled up two glasses. 'Here.' He slid them towards the girls. 'Turn that frown upside down, girl. He aint worth it.'

Alice picked up the glass and took a large gulp. 'Let's get shitfaced,' she announced to Sarah, who looked at her nervously.

'That's more like it. Wahey!' rejoiced Phil. He gave a quick glance in Hannah's direction just as she was knocking back her glass of wine and made her way out of the pub. 'Must be a full moon out there tonight,' he muttered under his breath.

'What?' Sarah asked.

'Oh nothing. Top up?' Phil offered, grinning like a Cheshire Cat.

21

OLLIE & SKY

As the sun began to set over Royal Victoria Country Park, Sky and Ollie walked towards the shops in Netley. Sky was confident that she could buy the vodka but told Ollie to make himself scarce as he made them look younger. He went into the fish-and-chip shop a few doors along and bought them a big portion of chunky traditional seaside chips to share. His mouth salivated as the rotund man behind the counter sprinkled salt all over them and gave a good squeeze of vinegar. As he was handed the warm bundle, his eyes dilated with pure pleasure. He inhaled the delicious aroma deeply and he couldn't wait to get stuck in.

Outside the shop, Sky was casually reading the bus timetable. As Ollie approached, she started moving ahead. She was behaving quite strangely he thought. They crossed the road and headed for the shingle beach.

'Why are you racing ahead? Wait for me.' He laughed as he walked briskly to try and keep up.

They found a spot and Sky was beaming and jumping up and down.

'I got served.' She shook her rucksack at him and

opened it up to reveal a bottle of vodka and some cans of fizzy mixers.

'So, did I,' said Ollie, shaking the portion of chips in front of them, both of them enjoying deep wafts of the salty, vinegary fumes.

'Oh my God, they smell so good. Let's get stuck in.' She laid out a fleece blanket that she had packed and sat down on the stones. 'Bit lumpy on the old bum, eh? Give me those. They smell ah-may-zing.'

The pair watched the sun set across the old refinery site ahead of them beyond the water, with just a bag of chips between them. Occasionally, Ollie would wait for Sky to pick a chip so that he could go in at the same time and 'accidentally' brush hands with her. He felt like something was brewing. She was very relaxed around him and yet he felt like he couldn't read her at all sometimes. As they talked and joked around together, he couldn't stop staring at her when she threw her head back and laughed. The dusk lighting created a silhouette of her womanly figure. *If only she would give me the come on. I think she wants me. God, I want her.* As he tried to not get caught staring at her, he found himself biting his lip and imagining his mouth on hers.

They had had a couple of large vodka and Cokes each when Sky suggested they put on some music on one of their phones. Ollie tossed his over to her and she started scrolling for music before deciding on a song and jumping up to dance to it.

She twirled and wriggled in the encroaching moonlight with the sea sparkling behind her as if pieces of tinfoil were randomly floating across its surface. She curled her index finger at Ollie and summoned his presence.

Reluctantly he joined her, not as keen to let himself go like she was. She took both of his hands and raised them up above them both and she slowly rocked and danced playfully in front of him. Ollie had no idea where to put his feet or his eyes, and felt like he wanted the dancing to end, or for her to pull him in. Occasionally, she would pull him closer before spinning him away. Each time she pulled him closer he would feel a rush of excitement, only to be strewn away again, like a yo-yo. He found the courage to meet her eyes and she held his stare, giving him an immediate erection. He was begging her silently to not look down. Suddenly, she pushed him away and burst into a fit of laughter.

'Why so serious! God, lighten up. If you can't dance silly with me, then who can you with?' She continued to twirl and glide about as she reached for the vodka and took a big, neat gulp. 'Uu-uurgh. It tastes like hairspray.'

'Well, it's not meant to be drank that way.' Ollie's mind was racing with uncertainty and an increasing desire for Sky. He needed to break what was happening before he embarrassed himself. 'Let's pack up and walk over to the ruins. I'd love to explore those for some photo ideas.'

'Sure.' Agreed Sky slightly stumbling back towards her bag. Ollie cleared his throat and tried to rub the frustration out of his hair. 'You need to drink more Oliver. Let yourself go a bit.'

'I uh ... I don't think that is a good idea.'

Sky was standing in front of him. She put her finger on his chest and poked him. 'Well, I demand it. Have more.' She gave him a wink and twirled again and was clearly very tipsy.

I think she wants me. I think something is going to happen. Take the drink and see what happens.

'Ok, pass it here. Stop hogging it then.' He took a swig and she cheered him on. He felt like he was coming to life. Excitement was running through his body and he was tingling all over. He watched her and let his mind wander, thinking what it would be like to touch her, and hoping she would touch him back.

As they left the beachfront, feeling full of courage, he put his arm around her waist and let his hand smooth her bum as a test to see if he was in with a chance.

'Oi you.' She laughed before linking arms with him to cross the road.

Something is going to happen. Tonight, she is going to give me her body and I am going to enjoy every minute of it. He let his imagination run wild.

As they got to the ruins, evening had arrived, and the velvet blue sky engulfed the castle ruins.

'I can't really make out good photo spots here. Shame, we will have to come back in daylight some-time,' suggested Ollie as he looked at Sky, tugging his sleeves over his knuckles.

'Yeah sure. I forget how quickly it gets dark at this time of year. We can come back anytime. Fancy a bifter instead?'

'What? Where did you get that?' asked Ollie in surprise.

'Nicked it from my mum, obviously,' said Sky nonchalantly.

'Why, obviously? I didn't realise your mum was a stoner?'

'She smokes it most evenings. Why do you think

she is so chill all the time? She is out of her box most of the time,' said Sky dismissively.

'Oh. I hadn't realised. I've never tried it before. I don't know if I want to. Plus, we've been drinking. Is it a good idea?' Ollie dug his hands deep in his pockets and shuffled his feet nervously as he watched Sky roll up.

'Don't worry, I'll make it mild. If you don't go mad, it gives you a nice trippy feeling when you've been drinking. We could spin out and watch the stars.'

'I don't know. I'm not sure if spinning out is my thing.'

'You'll love it and you're with me. You're safe.' She offered him a warm smile.

'Ok then. I guess I could try a tiny bit. But be gentle with me. Lol.'

'Oh, I'll be gentle with you alright.' She began sprinkling the weed into a long paper skin.

What does that mean? Is she planning on going the whole way with me tonight? Is she making us smoke weed so that we will both relax?

'In that case, let's do it. I am all yours, Miss Sky.'

'Ding-dong.' She winked.

Oh my God, we are going to do it. We are totally going to do it. Shit, I don't have any condoms. We could end up having sex and I don't have anything to use. Maybe she will wait until we are back at the house. As images of them together raced through his mind, his heart racing and his trousers feeling like they were going to burst, he leaned closer to her. He put his mouth on hers. *She's not pulling away. Oh my God, she is not pulling away.* He leaned on her harder and put a hand on her breast and squeezed it gently. She sat up. *Shit. Too far.*

'Easy, tiger.' She lit the joint and took a big drag before slowly exhaling and releasing a big grey cloud of smoke into the nearly black moonlit sky. She passed it to him without looking. 'Small toke. Don't suck too hard.'

What the fuck is happening here?

Ollie took a gentle toke and felt the drug work its way through his body, wondering what it was going to do to it. Partially afraid, partially excited. He wanted so desperately to kiss Sky again but was so confused as to if that was ok. She held her hand up next to him, summoning back the joint. He passed it to her and lay back down next to her. She put her hand on his leg and stroked it gently. The she passed the joint back. He took it and again inhaled just a small amount. She continued to stroke his leg and he did nothing to stop it. He passed the joint back to her and rolled onto his side. As she took the joint, he leaned in and kissed her neck.

I swear she moaned. He kissed it again, and then sucked gently. *She's moaning. She's definitely moaning.* He moved his mouth down onto her chest. He kissed and licked her and was about to pull her top down when she gently pushed him off and gave him the joint back.

What the fuck is happening? Does she want me? Is this just what stoners do? Does she want me to try harder?

22

HANNAH & CRAIG

Hannah trudged her way back home begrudgingly. She did not want to go there, but the only thing that felt good right now was lying in her big soft bed. She couldn't wait to pull the blankets up to her chin, put on Netflix, and drown out the thoughts and feelings of heartbreak. She prayed that Craig wouldn't be there when she got back. He was the last person she wanted to see.

Phil had gone out to empty the ashtrays and spotted Hannah dragging her heels down the woodland lane. Some criminal thoughts entered his mind; he was too out of shape to catch up with her and act out his thoughts. Still, the thought of grabbing her turned him on. It had been such a long time since he had been with a woman.

Hannah's heart sank when she saw the reflection of the television on through the window. Slowly, she turned her key in the lock, knowing that seeing Craig was inevitable but wanting to delay it for as long as possible. Quietly, she put her keys on the counter and slipped off her shoes. She felt a presence appear in front of her and she stowed her shoes away.

'You're back.' He stood there sheepishly, arms folded.

'Yes. Sorry to disappoint you.' She pushed past him into the kitchen and headed straight for the fridge.

'I'm not disappointed. I've been worried. I guess we need to talk.'

'We don't actually.' She pushed past again, carrying a wine glass and a bottle of wine. 'Just file for divorce. I'll agree to whatever you want.'

She sloped upstairs, leaving Craig perplexed by her placatory manner. He had been dreading her returning and the shouting and screaming even though he knew he deserved it, but this was worse. This, he had not expected.

———

The next morning, Hannah went downstairs and made no regard for a sleeping husband on the sofa. She banged about, opening and closing cupboards with more force than normal, putting away the dishes fairly noisily.

'Ok, ok, I get it. You don't need to make that much noise. I'm getting up,' he said accusingly.

'I'm not deliberately making noise. I'm just not deliberately being quiet,' she said dismissively.

'Hannah ... you must be thinking a thousand thoughts. Let's get this out in the open.'

'No, thank you. If you hadn't got things out in the open, like your penis, we wouldn't need to have this conversation. Uu-urgh ... it hurts to even think about it. I don't want to know. I don't want to picture it. Every time I close my eyes I see you with her. I see

you betraying me. I see you touching another. I just ...
I just ...

'How could you do this? I just wanted a baby. I wanted us to be a family. I was trying to extend our family, and the whole time you were tearing it apart. Like I said last night, let's just get divorced. You married the wrong woman, clearly. Come on, walkies.'

Their chocolate lab bounded over, and she clipped on her lead, stuffed some bags into her pocket, and left Craig standing there, speechless, again. As she turned the latch on the door, he ran towards her and grabbed her by the arms.

'We are not getting divorced. We are married. We work at this. We made vows,' he pleaded.

'Which you broke.' She yanked away her arm from him and felt a sharp pain in her abdomen on the right - hand side that brought her to her knees.

'Hannah!' Craig panicked. 'What's wrong?'

Hannah stood up carefully.

'You look like you've seen a ghost. Let's go to A&E.'

She yanked herself free from him again.

'I'm fine. Just fuck off, Craig. I don't want your pity.'

Hannah walked off with the dog, wondering what the sharp pain was in her side. It had become a dull ache now. Perhaps she had just pulled a muscle, she told herself. Despite telling herself it was nothing, she felt anxious, as if something might be wrong.

When she got home, she went to the loo and noticed there was dark blood coming from her. She wasn't meant to be on her period. *Perhaps I do need to phone the doctor. Am I having a miscarriage? I have already had my period since I last had sex.* She began to worry.

————

The next morning, she called the doctor and was able to get an emergency appointment, annoyed it was at the cost of sharing private information with an invasive receptionist. She flicked through an old magazine in the waiting room, wondering what was happening to her. The bleeding hadn't stopped. *What if it's cancer?*

She gulped down her fears. That little agreement with the sperm donor was a crazy thing to do. *What if he has given me a disease? I don't know anything about him.* She shuddered with shame when she thought back to how wild she had been with that man. A stranger. As she waited to be called in, she realised she felt so empty and so sad. No baby. A failed marriage.

The doctor called her name, and she offered a fake smile and made her way to his room. 'Hannah. How is it that I can help you today?'

'I seem to be bleeding when it is not time for me to have a period.'

'Really? What colour is the blood?'

'It's dark. Really dark. Not like a normal period.'

'When was your last period?'

'Just over two weeks ago.'

'And how long has this bleed been going on for?'

'It's been a few days, maybe longer. I've not really been paying attention. I've had a lot on my mind.'

'Hannah, have you done a pregnancy test?'

'No. I'm bleeding, so I assumed that I would not be.'

'I think you should go home and do a test and call me with the result. Any other issues?'

'No, not that I can think of. Actually, I did have a sharp pain yesterday. You really think I need to do a test?'

'It might be that you are having a miscarriage. We just need to rule some things out.'

Hannah looked down and began picking at her nails.

'So, if I am pregnant, it's likely that it's a miscarriage? I can't be pregnant, and it be ok?'

'I don't think so, Hannah. Call me when you've done the test.'

Once home, Hannah ran to the upstairs bathroom, bypassing Craig in the living room and ripped the test packet open. There was a small part of her that was hoping the doctor was wrong and that maybe she was pregnant and just experiencing some implantation bleeding or something. She peed on the stick and it came up immediately. Pregnant. Her heart fluttered into life as she gasped in awe at the stick. Excitedly, she ran into the bedroom and called the doctor to let him know.

Hearing the joy in her voice, he reminded her that she was likely having a miscarriage and that she needed to come in first thing and have a blood test to measure the pregnancy hormone in her body. This went on for three days. The first day the number was high. The second day it had dropped, but on the third day it had shot back up again. He called the hospital in front of her.

'I have a patient I am sending in. She has a positive pregnancy test with variable blood test results. I'd like her to have an urgent scan. Thank you.' He put the phone down and turned back to Hannah. 'You need to make your way to Princess Anne Hospital. The early pregnancy unit are expecting you. Oh, and Hannah. Don't go by yourself. Take someone with you.'

Hannah walked out of the surgery that day in a daze. She couldn't really understand what was happening. Why such a fuss over a miscarriage? Wouldn't it just bleed out? She called Craig and he didn't answer. They had barely spoken in the last week. She had been giving him the silent treatment whilst she came to terms with what was happening.

'Craig it's me. I'm pregnant. But I am having a miscarriage. The doctor has ordered me to go to the hospital. I am going there now.' She put the phone down, disappointed that he hadn't answered, but pulled herself together and headed towards the hospital.

Once there, she was seen fairly quickly, still completely bemused by how seriously she was being treated. There had been two other girls waiting, but once she arrived and told reception, she was called up right away. She went into a small consultation room and explained what she had said to the doctor. She had a normal period that had come and gone and now she was seemingly having another one. She had done a pregnancy test and it had been positive, the doctor had taken blood tests for three days and the pregnancy hormone was fluctuating, so she must be having a miscarriage. The nurse made lots of notes before telling her to follow her into another room.

'Pop your bag down on the chair over there. We

are going to do an ultrasound to figure out what is going on. So, bottom half off please and pop up onto the bed when you're ready.'

Hannah noticed how matter-of-fact the nurse was being. Her bedside manner needed some work. Hannah obliged and tried to remove her trousers discreetly.

'Use this sheet for your modesty. Just going to apply this cold gel and then I'll be ready if you are.'

Hannah nodded accordingly. Her eyes glued to the nurse, looking for any kind of giveaway as to what was happening. The nurse squinted. Then paused. Then rolled the scanner around a little more and stopped.

'Be back in a minute.'

Just like that she was gone. *What the hell is going on? How much examination does a miscarriage need?* Before she had more time to ponder that thought, the nurse was back with two colleagues. They all looked at the screen and pointed at something, and then whispered. They all then moved away from the screen and huddled in the corner to whisper some more. Hannah was about to lose her patience before the pack broke and stood around her.

'Hannah, you have what we call a pregnancy of unknown location. Are you not in tremendous pain?'

'So, a miscarriage then? No not really. The odd grumble.'

'Hannah, you are having an ectopic pregnancy. This pregnancy cannot survive, and we need to operate to remove the fetus.'

Hannah couldn't really grasp what she was being told.

'Operate? When? I will have to see when I can book some time off work.'

'Hannah. The pregnancy has become stuck in your fallopian tube and has ripped it. Your bleeding is not a period. It's internal bleeding. Had you left this any longer, you could have died. We are sending you to theatre now.'

Hannah's mouth fell open.

'Um, ok. I ... I need to phone my husband.'

'Yes, we advise you do. You will need to stay in overnight, but it would be good for you to have someone here, if he can get here in time. Do you have any questions, Hannah?'

'Yes, yes, I do actually. How far gone was I? Four weeks?'

'Looking at the measurements, you conceived ten weeks ago; hence, the tube being ruptured. It got stuck and it has ripped the tube. We will try and save the ovary. Hannah, we will need you to sign a consent form to say that you agree to the fetus being cremated.'

Hannah nodded in agreement as if in a trance. Still in a daze, she picked up her mobile and dialled Craig. It went straight to voicemail. *For fuck's sake.*

'Craig. It's me.' She began to sob. 'I am going into surgery. I am having an ectopic pregnancy.' She hung up and let the phone slip out of her hand onto the bed as the tears began to roll.

What seemed like ten minutes later, Hannah was on the bed, in her gown, and on her way into theatre.

'Sharp scratch. That's it. Just relax and count to ten for me. You're doing really well.'

Hannah winced as the needle was pushed into the canula. She thought she would play a game with the anaesthetic and beat it. She tried counting really quickly to ten. The room around her shrunk and her eyes closed at seven.

When Hannah awoke, she was wheeled back to her room very much in and out of a confused state. Craig was in the room, waiting for her. He leapt out of the chair and rushed to her side, picking up her hand in his and kissing the top of it.

'Hannah, I am so sorry. I am so sorry. I should've been here. You shouldn't have been on your own.'

Hannah rolled away from him and rested her head on her hands, sinking into the pillow. Silent tears streamed down her cheeks.

'Look, I know now is not the time ...' Craig, although concerned for Hannah, was elated that they had managed to conceive; the doctors had been wrong, he told himself. 'When you are better, we can try again. Now, we know we can do this. Let's get you better and then let's really try for this. Let's put our recent troubles behind us. It was the wake-up call I needed. Let's try for a baby.'

'It wasn't yours,' she murmured.

'What? What do you mean it wasn't mine?'

'It was mine. Only mine.' Hannah closed her eyes and fell back to sleep.

Craig looked on, dumbfounded.

23

ALICE & PHIL, OLLIE & SKY,
HANNAH & CRAIG

Alice had fallen completely off the wagon. The wagon was in bits. So broken that it could be sold as woodfire kindling. All the efforts of the last few months had gone out of the window.

Dan played around and around in her head like some 1970s record, images of him with a slight crackle to them dancing around in her mind. The only way to block the images, the memories, the good, the bad, was to numb her mind. She wasn't even trying to take it easy now. She wanted to get blind drunk every day. She signed herself off sick for a week with stress, and the drinking was creeping in earlier and earlier.

The other day it was three P.M. in the afternoon and yesterday it was midday. Quite a jump forward in time. An additional three hours of drinking but the hangover misery was making the pain of Dan's new romance unbearable to deal with, and she needed that numbing agent more and more each day.

Going to that rotten boozer the other day had turned out to be a dream. The sad old landlord who was so desperate to get a girl's attention would ply her with alcohol and for very little cost. She knew what she was doing. It would be unfair to say she was using him as this was a two-way transaction. He was very much bribing her with alcohol.

Steve, the kitchen cook had escorted her home last night, not that she remembered it, but she had a text on her phone from Sarah saying that she hoped she was ok and to remember to thank Steve when she saw him next. She had typed some drunken illogical nonsense back.

She knew very well that once she had made her way through this afternoon's bottle of wine, she would have a nap, freshen up, and make her way to the pub for more booze.

At the back of her mind, she knew this had to stop but she also knew this was a self-destruct episode that would last another couple of days. She had always managed to pull herself out of it and had decided not to fight her cravings. Life was miserable enough without having to battle with addiction. She would sort her life out next week, she told herself. For now, she was dealing with the pain of Dan's new chapter. She just needed to get over that initial discomfort, and then get back on track. *Besides, it's not like I am hurting anyone.*

Today, Alice opted for breakfast wine. She had never gone to that extreme before but had decided that if she was going to have a radical overhaul next week, she might as well go out with a bang. She might as well stoop as low as she could because this was rock bottom. She was going to be swimming to the shiny surface on Sunday, breaking through the turquoise water, sun beating down on her salt-cleansed skin, ready to get her life in order. That was how she pictured the metaphoric rise anyway ... metaphorically of course.

She felt quite excited about opening the wine for breakfast. This was new territory and like every addict, it was quite hard to get a buzz now, but this was new. This was naughty. This was reckless. This would be frowned upon by anyone that knew her, and she loved it. She savoured every moment. The cold feel on her fingertips of the chilled bottle. The crack of the seal as she unscrewed the cap.

'No. This is actually quite bad. Water first.' Putting the cold bottle on the worktop, she reached up to the cupboard for a pint glass. It was one that had been stolen on a night out once, obviously. It was a goblet style glass. She filled it up with tap water and guzzled it down. 'Aaaah. That's better. See, I am a good person.' Having a glass of water gave her the pass she needed to continue with her plan. She poured the glass and enjoyed the sound of the glug-glug from the bottle as the glass filled. For a moment, she stared at it and began to feel liberated.

'What do I have to be so miserable about? There are so many more that have a worse life than me. Here I am, no one is hurting me. I can drink wine whenever I like. In fact, seeing as I am going to go T—Total next week—today I am going to do whatever I like. I am giving myself the best send-off I can think of. Starting with this.' She picked up the glass and raised it high and in front of her. 'Cheers. This one is for you.'

In four large gulps, she downed the glass. 'Let's party. Whoop.' She poured another large glass and put some music on and began to dance in the kitchen. She was grabbing life by the balls and had decided from this day on, Dan was no longer going to control her life.

After the third glass, Alice began to feel a bit sleepy. It wasn't even midday yet after all. She took herself back to bed and put the TV on. All the curtains were still closed and the novelty of breaking a rule at nine A.M. that morning was suddenly not as liberating.

Come on Alice, you know how this works by now. Don't go to bed or you will feel sad all day. Sleep it off for an hour then get up and get out. Stop wasting your life. After her little pep talk, she knocked back the wine and went to sleep, knowing that as soon as she woke up, she would get showered and dressed and head to the pub to take advantage of the pervy landlord.

———

Phil had finished his morning routine of smothering himself using baby oil from a dusty old bottle whilst scrolling through Alice's photos online. He had ventured beyond her holiday photos and had found some of her when she was in secondary school. He particularly liked these photos. They reminded him of when he was a PE teacher and the teenagers had to do as they were told. They listened to him. They respected him. Lyndsey in particular. She had led him on. If it hadn't been for her, he wouldn't have ended up as this overweight old loser in a squalid bedsit above a run-down pub, he told himself. He shook the thoughts out of his head and zoomed in on Alice, tugging furiously at himself for his morning relief.

He was disrupted by a loud banging at the door.

'Fuck sake. Can a man not shoot his load these days?' He pulled his stained jogging bottoms up over his hard on and attempted to walk over to the door.

It was Steve. Phil let him in and walked back into the flat, scratching his arse. Steve had noticed the hard on and as he made his way into the flat and looking at the mess that surrounded him, he clocked Alice's profile on his laptop. He frowned and shuddered in disgust as he tried to keep his mind free from what he had just walked in on. The dog was staring at him and it appeared to have peanut butter around its mouth. Steve's eyes darted around the living room taking in one gross thing after another. Then he noticed the jar of peanut butter with a butter knife on top of it on the coffee table next to where the laptop was. He closed his eyes and shuddered. *No, not even Phil can be that wrong, surely.*

'I've just popped round to tell you I can't work tonight, sorry. Emma is ill and has asked me to have Sophie.'

'Whatever, just put a note on the website saying the kitchen it shut.'

'Can't you run the kitchen for one night?'

'On a Friday? Are you having a laugh? The bar will be filled with totty, and I want to be in the thick of it.'

'Ok, Phil,' said Steve, taking one last look around. 'If you're sure. I'll put the menus away. I'm surprised we can afford to miss out, but if you say so.'

'I do fucking say so actually, and it's your fault not mine. Take the night off ... unpaid.'

Steve shook his head and look around at the filth once more. 'You know what, Phil? I am the only one who has ever stood by you. If it wasn't for me, you wouldn't have a pub. You could've put extra staff on the bar tonight and you run the kitchen. You're wasting your life, Phil, and sort this shithole out. It's disgusting.'

Phil watched as Steve left, slamming the door behind him in frustration.

———

Ollie and Sky had not spoken about what had happened in Netley that night, much to Ollie's annoyance. It seemed to him that every time he tried to bring it up, Sky changed the conversation. She acted as though nothing had happened, despite Ollie believing they were close to having sex. Things had happened between them. Things she didn't put a stop to and, for the first time in months, he had felt joy and excitement run through him. Now, he was down and he felt more miserable than he could care to remember. The way she was acting made him wish that nothing had happened at all. He had gone from hoping to wondering, and it was driving him crazy. He decided that he was going to confront her and make her talk about it. He needed to know where he stood. That evening they had shared together made him the happiest he had been since the death of his mother. He closed his eyes to relive the moment and images of her throwing her head back laughing appeared. The vision of her body, her back arched, breasts pushed forwards, one leg bent at the knee with only the moon for light. It would've been so easy to roll over and hover over her ... slowly going in for the kiss, gently putting his lips on hers. She would welcome him and embrace him, kissing him like he'd never been kissed before, and then start tugging at his belt.

The clattering of cups from the kitchen broke him out of his trance. Someone was emptying the dishwasher. He sat up in bed with determination. He was going to confront Sky and ask her how she felt. He had to know. Good or bad, whatever the outcome, he had to know. Anything had to be better than not knowing, he concluded.

Ollie tiptoed downstairs and watched through the crack of the dining room door. Sky was enjoying a buttery crumpet whilst scrolling through her phone with her headphones in. Suddenly, he wanted to step back and leave it. If she wanted him, she would have told him? *Surely, unless, she was scared too?* Before he could step back, she saw him and pulled an earphone out of one ear.

'What are you doing you, weirdo?' she joked.

'I um ... I just uh ...'

'Come, sit down.' She pulled out the other earphone and put the phone down. 'Crumpet?' She slid her leftovers towards him.

Ollie bit his lip, crossed his arms, and looked around for anyone listening.

'What's going on? You look worried.'

Running his hand through his hair, Ollie slowly walked to the breakfast bar to sit next to her. The chair screeching as he pulled it out seemed irritatingly loud. 'Sky. Look, the other night.'

Sky dropped her head and went to pick up her phone.

Ollie, noting the signal, decided to bottle it.

She cleared her throat and pushed her phone further away. 'I thought this might come up. What about the other night?'

Ollie's mouth suddenly dried up, as if he had gone without water for days. 'Don't you think we should talk about it?'

Sky looked away. 'What is there to talk about?'

Ollie's frustration rose. He felt his fists clench and his heart begin to pound. He had opened the can and now he had to follow through. He wanted his feelings to be acknowledged. 'Well, there is plenty to talk about. What was it? I mean, what was it to you?'

Sky put down her crumpet and visibly swallowed a large lump and cleared her throat again. She leaned forward and put her hand on top of his. 'Ollie. Come on. Do we really need to have this conversation? Surely, you know we were just monged on weed and vodka?'

Ollie pulled his hand away swiftly and began pacing the kitchen.

Sky became flummoxed and uncomfortable. 'Ollie, babe ...'

'Don't. Do not call me babe.' He continued to pace whilst brushing his hair. 'So, it was nothing? Just a bit of fun with the sad little orphan?'

'Ollie ...'

'No, don't Ollie me. What was it? A sympathy touch-up? Try and boost my self-esteem? Because if that is what it was, then I really don't feel great now.'

'Ollie—'

'No, Sky! No. I thought you were one of the best. Too good for me? Yes. Way out of my league? Of course. I have been obsessed with you since the moment I met you and never in my wildest dreams thought we could be anything but the other night, the drugs, the alcohol ... I don't know ... but for a moment, you let me think we could be *something*. Is that just what you do? A little joint and a drink, and you're anyone's?'

Sky stood up, her chair screeching louder than his did. 'That is not fair.' She went to blurt out something, then hesitated. She looked down and began picking at her fingernails. 'Ollie, I'm gay. I thought you knew that and if I'm honest, I actually thought you were too.'

They both froze to the spot, Ollie's world crashing around him, thousands of memories flashing through his mind for what he had missed.

'Gay? You are *gay*?' he asked, almost choking on his own disbelief. 'And me? What? How? Why on earth did you think that?' He grew flustered. His face turned crimson. The pacing began again. He started to speak several times and lost the words he was trying to find.

'I had always thought we were two lost souls, not quite ready to come out, but supporting each other in our own little way as we came to terms with who we are,' Sky said, reaching out, trying to touch Ollie.

He flinched and pulled away. 'I am not gay.' He held her stare before storming off, closing the door very loudly behind him.

Sky, left standing, feeling hopeless and guilty for leading him on.

He ran up to the room. The blood rushing to his head. He grabbed his backpack from under the bed and began frantically packing items into it, not really checking what they were. As he opened the bedroom door, squeezing his feet into his tied-up pumps, he hobbled back to the bedside table and grabbed his camera. Then he thundered down the stairs, whizzing past the kitchen determined not to be stopped, and heard the faint cries of Sky calling him as he slammed the front door and stormed across the shingle driveway.

Ollie meandered his way through Woolston and headed for Netley. He didn't really want to go there because last time he was there he'd thought something was beginning with him and Sky. Now, he knew that she was using him until she could find the courage to be with a woman. He had never felt so low in his life. Being used was one thing but being used by someone who didn't even want a man was something he couldn't get his head around. *And she thought I was gay? Why? What do I do that is gay?*

He kicked a pebble that was in front of him and watched it hop further along the pavement. He went into a backstreet off-licence and got himself a small bottle of vodka. Those small independent ones never asked for ID. As long as you were polite, gave the nod and were discreet, you could buy alcohol and cigarettes, no questions asked. Ollie shoved the small bottle of vodka into the inside pocket of his coat and carried on his unplanned journey. His phone beeped. It was Sky.

'I didn't mean to upset you. I thought we were best friends, xx.'

Ollie shoved his phone back into his pocket and carried on his disgruntled way.

———

Alice was in a great mood. She was half a bottle of wine in. She had had a shower. The tunes were on, and she was looking forward to an afternoon in the pub, getting free booze from the fat old pervy landlord. She put on a flimsy dress. It was a bit boho. Not much to the material, a gingham pattern. She paired it with a cropped denim jacket and she slid on some converse pumps. She examined her look in the floor-length mirror and felt quite pleased with herself. Given how badly she had been treating her body lately, she didn't look too bad. Either that or the concealer was as good as it claimed to be. She smoothed a slick of raspberry red lipstick across her lips, blotted them together and pouted in the mirror, ignoring the voices in her head that were questioning her excitement about having drinks with no one, nothing arranged, apart from a sad old loser that fancied a piece.

Craig drove Hannah home in silence. After she had awoken from her announcement, he had asked her if she was ok, but she ignored him and tried to get out of the bed, which was clearly painful for her to do. He had reached out to help her and she pushed him off. She delicately got up and began packing up her bag. She asked him to take her home and exited the hospital bedroom ahead of him. He walked closely behind her, head spinning with thoughts. He wondered if she had just said it out of rage. *Surely, she hasn't been with another man? She isn't the type. She's just angry.*

The silence in the car was deafening. Craig hated

it whenever Hannah got mad, but this was worse. He just wanted to know what was going to happen next. Were they really over? He regretted his affair so much and wanted desperately to care for Hannah. He knew how much the ectopic would've been a blow to her. That was the closest she had got to her dream, and it nearly cost her life, and the baby was not meant to be.

'Look, Hannah. Let's go home. You can put your feet up and let me take care of you. I can make this right. This has been a wake-up call for both of us. I know I have hurt you, but I promise you, it meant nothing. We can talk when you are ready but until then, just let me look after you, and I promise I will do everything I can, that you need, to feel comfortable.'

He reached his hand over to hers and squeezed it. She reciprocated, and Craig felt relief, and hope wash over his body.

———

Alice made her way down to the pub, feeling the happiest she had for a while. She was looking forward to a day free of booze before getting her life back on track tomorrow. A last hurrah. One more day of feeding the problem, but she was going to enjoy it, make the most of it, and go out with a bang. Maybe even give herself a hangover so bad that she would never want to drink again.

She took a deep breath as she pushed the pub door open knowing that she was saying goodbye to the poison once and for all ... tomorrow.

"Ello, gorgeous. I didn't realise I was getting to see you today. Fancy a drink?'

'Oh, go on then'—she blushed—'would be rude

not to.' She got her empty coin purse out of her pocket and began fumbling with it.

'You can put that away. This is on me.' He winked at her and her stomach knotted.

'Only if you're sure,' she replied coyishly.

'You're the only one in here, you're keeping me company. I'd even go so far to say we are mates now.'

Alice smiled nervously and put away her purse. Scared by the game she was playing but excited for the free booze.

Phil handed her a large glass of cheap rosé. 'Might as well start as we mean to go on, eh. Chin-chin.'

They clinked glasses.

'Steve has taken the day off today; otherwise, I'd offer to do us some lunch. Want some crisps or something?'

'No, it's ok, thanks. Eating is cheating as they say,' replied Alice, trying to meet his eyes but found herself looking at the floor and feeling uncomfortable.

'Good girl,' said Phil, not being discreet as he eyeballed her up and down.

Ollie skulked his way through Netley village, feeling very sorry for himself. He had made light work of that small bottle of vodka and had smoked his way through most of the cigarettes. He was wracking his brain for evidence that he might've missed. How could he have *not* noticed she was gay?

As he rattled his way through old conversations, he recalled how she always complimented women on their style or told them they had nice hair or that she liked their lipstick. He had just thought she was being friendly. He liked that about her. That she was nice to other girls. He hadn't realised she had been flirting with them. The more he thought about it, the more he realised he had never heard her say she fancied a boy. Maybe it was obvious, but it hadn't been to him. Was it because he liked her so much that he had created a version of her to suit his own needs?

Now that he was looking back, was their relationship real or had he put rose-tinted spectacles on it? He sat down on the grass verge and put his head in his hands. He felt so stupid and to make matters worse, not only had he lost what he thought could've been a romance, he had now lost a friend and probably his accommodation. If only they hadn't got wrecked together that night, none of this would've happened and they could've still been friends. *But she came on to me, she led me on, she acted like she wanted it. We nearly had sex.*

He tossed a bit of litter away in frustration. He was angry now. She had used him and he was the one left feeling stupid. She was not the kind girl he had thought she was. He quickly stood up and marched over to the off-license. He sauntered up to the till and requested cigarettes and vodka.

The man behind the till looked at him quizzically.

'Please, don't. I am not having a good day. Help a brother out.'

The fifty-something-year-old man looked at him sympathetically. 'Girl trouble?'

'Yes,' said Ollie, looking down at the ground.

'Ok, I 'll sell it to you today, but take my advice. You're allowed to have an off day. Drown your sorrows, but only for one day. You do it for two days, it becomes a habit. So, drink it down, cry it out, and then pick yourself back up again.'

'Thanks, I really appreciate that.'

They exchanged goods and Ollie turned on his heels and headed for the beach.

———

Steve arrived for his shift at the pub and was disappointed to see Alice propping up the bar to a clearly delighted Phil. Steve greeted them both, rolled his eyes at Phil, and made his way into the kitchen.

'Thought you couldn't do tonight, Steve?' Phil hollered after him. 'Can't keep away from me, can you?' Phil started to laugh and looked at Alice for her reaction before bursting into a coughing fit, almost retching as he tried to regain his composure.

Alice and Phil were already a few drinks in and it was going to Alice's head quicker than Phil's.

'Come on, you're not a light-weight, are you?'

'I didn't think so, but I am giving it up tomorrow.'

'What? Why? That's crazy talk. Where is the fun in that?' Phil could see the images of Alice in his head that he had been hoping for slowly disappearing out of reach.

'My life is a mess. I am a mess. I need to sort my shit out and this stuff, as much as I love it, is the Devil's juice.'

'Hmmm ... so, this is your last soiree for a while. Fancy ramping things up a bit?'

He had caught Alice's attention now. She looked right at him.

'What are you thinking?'

Phil put his hand in his pocket and pulled out a little white bag of powder and put it in front of her.

'Coke?'

'Yeah. Let's make this last party count.'

He stared at her, hoping she would accept, and he could get her wrecked and then who knew what that could lead to. Alice touched the bag. 'Go on, take it. Go to the loo and snort your life out,' said Phil, belly-laughing to himself.

'I've never done it before. What will it be like?'

'It's nothing, really. All a load of hype. It just keeps you straight if you want to drink all day. Here, I'll rack up a small one here and see if you like it.'

Phil opened the small bag and tipped out a small amount of the powder. He pulled his wallet out of his back pocket and retrieved a card. Quickly and neatly, he made a little white line with the powder and then rolled up a note and handed it to her. 'Go on. Try it.'

She looked at him nervously.

'A small amount like that won't do anything.'

Alice took the note, leaned over the powder, and sniffed it up.

'Anyone would think you have done this before. Done like a true professional.'

'I've watched a lot of films.' Alice rubbed her nose as it tickled and then felt it drop down the back. She grimaced. 'Uu-urgh, it tastes disgusting.'

Phil slid the glass of wine towards her and watched her take a sip.

'Good girl.' He winked at her and she could sense that today was going to get messy.

———

Craig and Hannah arrived home and he cradled her into the house. Gently, he guided her into the living room and eased her on the sofa. He tenderly put a cushion behind her head and put a blanket over her. He handed her the TV remote and stroked her hair. Slowly, he leaned down and delicately kissed her on her forehead.

'What would you like? Cup of tea?' he asked lovingly as he stroked her arm.

'Wine.'

'Do you rea—'

'I said wine.'

Craig stood and took his orders. He went to the kitchen and poured a glass of wine. He found some chocolates in the cupboard and carried them through to the living room. He passed the glass of wine to Hannah and then sat next to her on the edge of the sofa.

'Are we going to talk? I think we should.'

'I've just had a baby removed from me by surgery. I have had an ovary and fallopian tube removed. My chances of having a child have been slashed by half. I had to sign a form saying I was happy for the fetus to be cremated. You've been fucking a teenager. What *exactly* would you like to talk about?'

Craig put his head in his hands and sighed deeply. 'Ok, ok, I get it. But don't shut me out. We can work this out. I want to make this work with you, Hannah.'

Sulkily, Craig crept upstairs, taking a moment to stop and look at their wedding photos pinned to the wall. They had been so happy that day, it really had been one of the best days of his life. He didn't want these pictures to become meaningless. He didn't want them to be stored away in box in the loft. They had made promises to each other that day and he was going to start living up to them, from this day forward.

He lay down on the bed and got his phone out of his pocket. He looked up Hayley's number and began writing out a text underneath the several ones he had ignored from her in the recent days. She had gotten very angry and verbally abusive with him, not knowing what he and the wife he had betrayed had been going through. She had shown just how juvenile she was, expectedly so, but it was not something he could deal with. Hannah needed him, and that was where he wanted to be.

'Hayley, I am sorry I haven't been in touch. Something terrible has happened at home. I can't do this with you anymore. I have betrayed my wife and she needs me now. She knows about us and she is willing to give me another chance. I have to take it. You are a lovely young woman and you will find your own husband one day. I am sorry. Take care.'

She began typing immediately and he had a feeling it was not going to be a sympathetic reply. He blocked her before she could finish whatever outburst she was about to launch at him.

Restless and anxious, he decided to go out and buy some nice things for Hannah. A care package—flowers, chocolates, one of those ridiculously expensive candles, some wine maybe. The idea of putting it all in a little basket made him smile to himself. He skipped down the stairs, into the living room, and kneeled next to Hannah.

'How are you feeling? You ok?'

She smiled an empty smile back at him.

'I'm going to go out to the shop and get some bits.

Is there anything you'd like me to get? I'm thinking of getting a few bits in, so we don't need to leave the house for the next few days. I'm taking some time off work so that I can look after you ... and uh, I don't know if this is the right timing, but I told Hayley I have no interest in her. I am with you and she was a mistake. I promise you, I am all yours and I will make this up to you. I am going to be the husband you married again.'

She gave him a gentle smile and rubbed his hand.

He felt a warm glow rise in him. 'I won't be long, baby. Text me if you think of anything.' He left quietly and Hannah rolled over and cuddled herself into the sofa, contemplating a fresh start with Craig.

———

Ollie kicked stones along the shore as he walked, unsure of what to do. He felt like he had made things so much worse. If he had left the conversation alone, he would still have a friend and a home. Now, he had nothing.

Suddenly, images of his mother on her deathbed flashed into his mind, and he felt himself wince in shame. He hadn't been focused when all of that was going on. He had been spinning figurative plates in his mind. His mother was dying, he was about to be a homeless orphan, but he could remember feeling like it would all be ok because he had Sky. Guilt raced through him that he should've been more attentive towards her, whether she was in a coma or not. He just didn't know how to deal with it and Sky had made it all seem like it was going to be ok. He'd latched onto that. To the comfort and security that she'd offered.

He sat down on the stones and unscrewed the bottle of vodka. He looked at it before tipping his head back and taking a big neat gulp. He screwed up his face and squeezed his eyes shut at how disgusting it tasted. He examined the bottle once more and went in again. This time shuddering as it laced his body with heat.

The sun was beginning to set. The bottle was half empty and he wasn't feeling numb enough. He retrieved a joint from his pocket. Sky had made it on that fateful night out, but they had ended up too stoned to have it. He kept it, almost knowing he would need it again at some point. He lit it up and took a long drag before coughing furiously. Once he got over the ripped throat, he began to embrace the mellow sensation running through him. He felt pretty messed up now. The vodka and the weed had created the perfect cocktail that he needed to block everything out.

Perhaps I could sleep on the beach tonight? Getting more annoyed at his own sulky behaviour, he gave himself a talking to and decided to try and snap out of it. *Something will come good. it has too. Life has been too hard recently.* He looked up at the moon. *Just give me a break for fuck's sake. Please. Make this situation good again. I can't take anymore.*

He pulled out his camera and took a picture of the white strips of moon blanketing the calm, rippling sea. He had taken a good picture. One of his best, so he decided to make the most of his evening and go about an evening photo shoot. He scooped up his bags, took one last long drag on his joint, and flicked it away from him. Wobbling as he stood, he felt his head spin and felt suitably numb for now.

———

Alice was three sheets to the wind and Phil was enjoying every minute of it. She was being tactile, laughing at his jokes, leaning into him on her bar stool. At least that was what he thought. She was highly intoxicated and swaying from side to side. Almost completely incoherent. The bar was filling up. Women looked disapprovingly. Men observed nonchalantly. Phil watched on very happily.

Steve came out of the kitchen and went behind the bar and made himself a pint of blackcurrant squash. He looked at Alice and then Phil and shook his head in disgust. Leaning over the bar, he spoke softly to Phil. 'This is not a good look, Phil. She is off her face. She needs to go home.'

'And who is going to take her? *This* is home by the looks of it. Certainly has been for the last few weeks anyway. She loves Phil's freebies.'

'Not exactly free, Phil. I think they are called bribes. She is in no fit state. Plus, she's about twenty years younger than you. Don't do anything stupid; this is a disaster waiting to happen.' He stared at Phil, waiting for some kind of acknowledgement, but all he got back was a sulky face.

'I mean it, Phil. Don't do anything.' He walked off, shaking his head, and carrying his pint of squash back to the kitchen.

Phil looked at Alice. She wasn't even holding her head up properly now. She was slouching, and the bar was definitely propping her up. As he examined her, he noticed the bag she was wearing just about hanging on to her shoulder. It was open enough for him to spot her car keys glinting through the opening. *Maybe I should make sure she gets home?*

He looked around him and felt himself getting sweaty with excitement. The pub was getting busy, but they were all talking amongst themselves. No one was paying attention to Alice at this moment. No one was looking at all.

He sidled up next to her and put her arm around his neck.

'Time to get you home love. You've had enough.' He hoisted her up off the chair and beckoned a bar maid over. 'Just putting her in a cab. Cover the bar please.' With that he staggered out carrying her dead weight around him as quickly but as discreetly as possible. Once in the car park, he got her keys out of her bag and pressed the unlock button. To his delight a car lit up and revealed itself and no one was around. Quickly, he dragged her to the car and slumped her into the passenger seat. He leaned over her to put her seatbelt on and took a good look down her top whilst he was there. Speedily, he ran around to the driver's side and put the key in the ignition. He revved up the engine and spun out of the car park in a puff of dust. The excitement was raging through him now. She was out cold, they were all alone and no one knew they were together.

He drove along at speed, meandering along the country lanes, recklessly swerving and observing that Alice was dead to the world. He found a lay by and pulled over. No one was coming. There were no lights. It was just him and the darkness. He switched the ignition off and licked his lips, feeling himself getting hard instantly. He went to kiss her on the mouth and thought better of it. He grabbed a breast, his hand shaking but it did not startle her. He undid the top buttons on her blouse and pulled one side of her bra down. Still nothing from Alice. He put his mouth on her and sucked. Still nothing. He began sucking and kissing her chest frantically. He wanted more but wasn't sure what he could get away with. He got out of the car and went around to her side. Looking around him he opened the door and lowered her seat as far as it would go. She was as close to a lying position as he could get her. He quickly pulled his trousers down, revealing his excitement. He climbed in and started pulling at her trousers. She twitched. He stopped, eyes locked on her, then stillness again. He tried to put his hand inside her pants, but her jeans were too tight. He was desperate now and so close to touching a real woman. He began tugging at her clothes trying to make enough room to get himself close enough to have sex with her. His heart was racing. His penis was throbbing. If he wasn't careful he could explode at any moment. He just wanted to get to her so desperately. He tried tugging at her clothes again and managed to get them down far enough. He lay on top of her and tried to spread her legs apart. She began to stir. He began to panic. He was so close to what he had wanted for so long. He could not miss out on this now. He tried to shove himself in and as he did he saw wide awake eyes looking right at him. He leapt off, hitting his head on the roof of her car and panicked. She looked confused.

'What? What are you doing? Get off of me.' She slurred.

He put a hand over her eyes and one around her throat.

'Shut up. Shut the fuck up.' She went to say something. 'Shut up or I will fucking kill you.' He swung a punch at her and knocked her out.

He ran around the car and got back into the driving seat. He turned the key and drove off at speed.

———

Ollie had taken some great pictures that night. The alcohol and cannabis were wearing off and he decided he was going to have to sleep rough tonight. He was scared and nervous, but he couldn't think or see ahead of him. He just needed to lie down and forget about it all. Every minute that passed that he hadn't heard from Sky left him feeling more and more exasperated. Dragging his feet along the road behind him, drained by the drama of everything, his eyes holding back the tears that were desperate to spill over he trudged along, wondering what he was going to do next. His options were extremely limited. He hoped that Sky would get in touch and tell him it would all be ok; if not he was going to run away, start a new life. A life as an orphan on the streets.

Realising he was running out of steam, he tossed his bag down onto the grass and fell down in a slumped heap. He looked up at the stars and begged for answers. He needed another option. Another way out of this turmoil he was entrenched in. He was scared. He was lost. He felt hopeless. His freezing cold fingers shook as he tried to unclip his backpack. *Maybe looking at the pictures I took today will make me feel better. Photography is my escape. Photos cap-*

ture true reality but create made up stories in an image.

He clenched his chattering teeth as he rummaged through his bag trying to find his camera; the dark evening that enveloped him made it difficult. He shook it out of frustration and as he did, his camera fell out and tumbled down the grass verge towards the road. He crawled down the grass embankment to try and stop it from going into the road. Headlights from the distance lit up the dark country lane. Suddenly, he was not surrounded by darkness anymore. He was being blinded by full beam headlights.

'No!' Ollie shouted as he saw his beloved possession roll to a stop in the middle of the road. Without thinking, he ran to grab it, not realising how fast the car was approaching. The impact was quick, and his body bounced over the bonnet before collapsing with a thud onto the road.

———

Phil screeched to a stop as the car zigzagged across the road. Both hands shaking furiously on the steering wheel. His body trembling. He looked in the rearview mirror and saw a mound on the road, not moving. Realising no one was around, he sped off towards Alice's house, leaving whatever it was he had hit in a heap on the road behind him.

Ollie's eyes flickered, not really understanding what had just happened. He saw the crescent of the moon and felt something trickle out of his ear before giving up and closing his eyes.

Craig drove along happily, knowing that Hannah was at home waiting for him. He was grateful for that at least. He tapped his fingers on the steering wheel along to the music on the radio and inhaled the waft of the Chinese take-away that he had just bought to take home to them both. As he cruised along he saw something in the road ahead. *What is that? Is it a deer? Jesus Christ, it's a body!* He slowed down, panicking at his discovery and trying to remain calm. He stopped a few yards before the person, not wanting to contaminate the crime scene or disrupt any evidence. He put on his hazards and jumped out. Frantically, he dialled 999 as he approached the body.

'Hello. Ambulance now. It's a ... it's a ...' He looked around the lifeless body. 'Oh shit, it's a child. Well, a young man.'

'Is the man breathing?'

'I'm too scared to touch him.' Craig was shaking and going into shock.

'Place a finger under his nose. See if you can feel any warm air coming out.'

'Yes. Yes, I think I can feel something but come quick. He is badly injured and there is blood. It looks like it is coming from his head.'

Craig liaised with call handler and spoke to them until help arrived. The pitch-black sombre lane was now illuminated with blue lights and emergency crew trying to save a life.

By the time Craig got home, Hannah was asleep on the sofa. She woke as he sat next to her and his face told her that something terrible had happened. He told her, in his state of shock, what he could remember.

'The worst thing about it, Hannah, is that as he lay in the road fighting for his life, his family will have been at home, not knowing how seriously hurt he was.'

Hannah pulled Craig into her and comforted him as he sobbed.

———

Phil brazenly walked back into the pub as Steve was closing up.

'Where have you been?' Steve asked suspiciously.

'Popped out to the cashpoint and ended up in Pete's bar for a bit,' replied Phil dismissively.

'And what about the girl? Alice? What happened to her?'

'I saw her into a taxi and she left. Who fucking asked you, anyway? Keep out of my business. I'm off to bed. Make yourself useful and fucking lock up, will you?' Phil threw his keys onto the bar and went to his flat upstairs.

Steve glared at Phil walking away as a horrible knot formed in his stomach.

———

Alice woke up feeling sick to her stomach. She knew something had happened. Something very bad had happened, but she didn't know what. She could hardly remember a thing. She was lying on her bed, on top of her blanket with all of her clothes on but her bottom half had been pulled low down enough. Enough for someone to get inside of her. She knew she had been assaulted. Her top had been interfered with too. She looked down and felt immediately un-clean. She didn't know how far the assault had gone.

She couldn't remember anything. She knew she had been at the pub, but that would have been hours ago. A huge chunk of time was missing.

She got up and felt a horrendous pounding at the front of her head. As she walked slowly towards the bathroom she saw herself in the mirror and noticed a large cut to her eyebrow. Nothing was making sense right now.

As she drenched herself in hot water in the shower, desperately trying to get herself clean and feel normal again, she was startled by a loud thumping on the door. Panicking, she stepped out of the shower and peaked out of the bathroom window. The frosted glass made it challenging to see but there was no denying the colours of white, blue and illuminous yellow that she could make out on the parked vehicle outside of the house. Her heart sank.

'Fuck.' She gulped heavily and wrapped her dressing gown around herself, and very nervously went to the door.

'Alice Baker?'

'Yes,' she whispered.

'We are going to need you to come with us to the station.'

'Why?'

'To be questioned over the hit and run of Ollie Stephens.'

The room darkened around her and she couldn't hear the police officer who was clearly speaking to her. She felt her legs go and she gave in to the darkness.

———

Sky began to worry that Ollie hadn't answered any of her calls or texts, and now he hadn't come back. She felt awful and she felt confused. There was something about Ollie, but she still hadn't figured herself out. She didn't know what she liked or who. She didn't know if she was gay or bisexual or what. All she knew was that she didn't want to lose Ollie as a friend.

She became restless and felt as though something was wrong. Pacing her bedroom and taking it in turns to look at her phone and look out of the window. She lay down on her bed and tried to put it to the back of her mind. Burying the niggly feeling as best as she could. She chewed frantically on her bottom lip as she opened Facebook on her phone and began scrolling through when a post caught her eye. A teenage boy had been involved in a hit and run and had been rushed to hospital. Police were appealing for witnesses. It was the road near their favourite spot in Netley Abbey.

Sky leapt out of bed and burst into her mum's bedroom. 'It's Ollie, I think he is hurt!'

———

The police tried questioning Alice, but she had closed up. She was ashamed to admit she couldn't remember a thing. *I must have done it. I just can't remember anything.*

'Alice, it would be in your interest to corporate. This is a really serious situation. The boy could die.'

Alice felt sick.

'Just tell us. What happened?'

'I-I,' Alice stammered. 'I c-can't remember.' The words coming out of her mouth like a faint whisper.

'Well, what do you remember? Start from the beginning of the day.'

'I just wanted to get drunk. I. Well, I think I might be an alcoholic.'

The two police officers swapped glances of concern.

'I wanted to spend the day getting drunk. I had said it was going to be my last time. I was going to clean my act up, starting today.' She looked down, examining the palms of her hands desperate for help.

'So, when you decided you were going to spend the day getting drunk, what were your plans? To do it alone or with someone else?'

'No. I had some wine at home but then I was going to go to The Red Lion.'

'The Red Lion in Netley?'

Alice gave a slow nod.

'Why there? To meet friends?'

'No. The landlord gives me free drinks.'

The police officers made some quick notes.

'I was going there for the free drinks.' She began to sob quietly and used her sleeve to wipe her nose.

'What's his name?'

'Phil.'

'And you and Phil are friends?'

'Not really. I started drinking there recently and he started giving me free drinks, so it became kind of a thing.'

'So, you go there on your own and get free drinks and drink alone?'

'No. Phil always sits with me. He'—she began to

cry harder—'I guess you could say having his company is part of the deal.'

'What is his company? Have you had sexual relations?'

'No! Well ...' Alice looked around the room, playing with her fingers, and looking anxiously around her.

'Alice, is something the matter? You can tell us anything you know. We are here to help.'

'Well, it's just that ...' She looked around her again and rubbed her palms up and down her thighs. 'When you came to my house, I wasn't long awake. I don't remember how I got home last night, but when I woke up, I wasn't dressed properly.'

The two policemen looked at each other again.

'What do you mean, you weren't dressed properly?'

'My clothes were on, but my trousers and pants had been pulled down to my knees and I woke up like that.' Alice began to cry heavily.

'Alice, do you think something happened to you last night?' Do you think you were assaulted?'

Alice nodded glumly, partly wishing she could remember and half wishing this nightmare would end.

Sky held Ollie's hand as she watched his weak chest moving up and down, wires coming out of him and machines bleeping. Her own heart was almost matching the pace of the bleeps that flooded the tense room with sound. Her stomach was churning with guilt and her mind racing with thoughts about how this could have been avoided. She wondered where he had been and what had to led to this moment. Part of her had wondered if he had deliberately got himself injured. She tried to tell herself that was madness, but he has been through so much and she knew he was not in a good place.

She took her phone out of her pocket and began scrolling through pictures of happier times. It seemed obvious to her now that he had feelings for her and that perhaps she had been careless, given his vulnerability. Suddenly, a thought appeared. *Where is his camera? That will tell me what he was doing last night.* She found his backpack stowed away down the side of the bed and she picked it up and looked through it. There was his wallet and some other personal items, but the camera was not there. She knew he wouldn't have gone out without it. She put his bag back under his bed and left his bay to find a nurse.

'Excuse me. Ollie's things? Where are they?'

'I think everything he had is with him. I know the police have been in to see him, but I don' think they took anything apart from the clothes he had been wearing.'

'There's a camera. There should be a camera. He takes it everywhere and takes photos of everything.'

'Sorry, I don't know,' said the nurse sympathetically. 'Maybe speak to the police and see if they have it?'

Sky dashed back to the bay and put a hand gently on Ollie's cheek.

'I'm going to find your camera. It might tell us what happened to you.' She gave him a peck and looked at him for a moment before leaving on a mission, determined to get to the bottom of this. Hoping and having a hunch, that the answer was on that camera.

Sky's mother picked her up from outside the hospital and they headed to the crash scene. Looking at it, you would never know that someone was fighting for their life. It was a normal country lane. Grassy verges, the odd puddle here and there, but absolutely nothing to tell you that the sky was flooded with blue lights last night as a young man was scraped off the road and rushed to intensive care.

Life goes on, Sky thought. She scoured the road but couldn't see anything. The road looked plain. Not even any litter lying around, never mind any clues. She went over to the verge on one side of the road and trod carefully on the grass, examining the area around her feet. She couldn't see anything and was getting frustrated. She just knew she was on to something. She had a feeling that something was here, and it was her job to find it. As if something was screaming silently at her.

She crossed the road and began scouring the other verge. She walked carefully up and down, up and down, but nothing. Irritated and defeated, she walked back to her mother's car and there it was. Just like that, she spotted something black in the grass. She ran over to it and was elated to find the camera. *Jackpot*. She picked it up and examined it. It was a little scratched but seemed intact. She got in to the car.

'I found it, Mum, I found it!' They both smiled nervously as Sky fiddled with it. 'It won't turn on. Let's take it home and see if it needs charging.'

'We should take it to the police.' Realising her daughter's determination and feeling quite proud of her, she winked. 'Ok, honey. Let's go.'

Sky put on her seat belt and cradled the camera in her lap as her mother drove them both back home. The journey seemed to take forever. Sky was tapping her foot in agitation.

Once home, Sky dashed into the house, leaving the front door wide open for her mum to close. She rifled through the kitchen drawer to find a charger that would fit the camera. She found something that looked right and frantically tried to slot it in, but was being so haphazard that her mother took it from her and gently placed the cable into the camera. A red light came on. Sky and her mother looked at each other.

'It won't come on any quicker by staring at it. It might even be broken. Or there might be nothing on it. I'll make us some tea. Go and sit in the front room and by the time we have had some tea, there should be enough charge on it to have a look. If ... it works that is.

Sky knew she was onto something. She couldn't put her finger on it, but she knew it was down to her to get that camera and the contents. The police had said they had arrested a woman, but something was bugging Sky. She didn't know what it was that she was looking for. Something in her head kept saying: *the, camera, find the camera.*

The air was thick with anxiety as the two women drank their tea. Sky was pacing the living room as her mother watched her nervously, wishing she could soothe her stressed daughter.

'Right, it must have some charge in it by now. Shall we go and look?' Sky wanted her mother with her but was unsure as to why.

'What is it that you think you are going to find,

darling? They have arrested a woman. What is it that is bothering you?' asked her mother in a soft tone.

'I don't know, Mum. Something just doesn't feel right. The whole evening was weird, and something is urging me to look at the camera. It is Ollie's prized possession and if he dies, what is on there will be the last documented moments of his life. I just want to see if he took anything and figure out where he was at in his head, you know?'

The light on the camera was green. Sky opened it and selected to look at the photos from the menu. She hurriedly went back to the beginning of the evening so that she could piece together his movements. He had gone back to Netley Abbey, he had sat on the shore and had some drinks. She managed to piece together that much. *So, was he drunk? Did he fall out onto the road?* Then the evening shots came. There were some of the moon highlighting the water again. Then there seemed to be some of passing cars. Taken as if he was lying on his belly on the verge, catching them as they approached or drove past.

'Hang on, Mum. This is the car that hit him. Didn't they say it was a navy estate car? Oh my God, there are more. The car is getting closer to him. This one is pitch black? Maybe it took a photo as he was hit by the car and it tossed into the air? Yes. That is the last one.'

Sky's mother was holding her shoulders, looking over at what he had captured. Sky started scrolling back.

'Wait. Stop,' said Sky's mum. 'Can you zoom in?'

'Why? Let me see.' Sky managed to zoom in, but the picture became slightly blurry.

'Oh my God,' Sky's mum gasped.

'What?'

'Sky, there are two people in that car and it is not the woman behind the wheel.'

Sky gasped and looked at her mother in disbelief, then at the image, and back at her mother.

'We need to take this to the police. That woman they have was *not* responsible for this.'

———

Alice hugged her knees and looked around the depressing, cold room that she had been locked up in. She had been taken to the medical ward where she had cried silently as they took a vaginal swab from her. She felt mortified. Not just because she was having to expose her body to be tested, but also because she just couldn't really remember anything. *How could I let myself get into such a state? This is all my fault. My stupid reckless behaviour got me sexually assaulted and put someone in an ambulance. I hate myself. I want to die.*

She rocked gently back and forth on the bed, holding her knees tight, trying to banish the images of the forensic testing, and willing her mind to tell her what had happened last night. All she could remember was being in the pub. Phil had given her cocaine. That was all she could muster. She scanned the room for ways to end it all. There was no point in living. Her family and friends would disown her once this got out and there would be no point in living. They would all think she was a drug user when it had only been that one time. They would never believe a thing she said again as they would just think she was a lying drug-taking idiot. She was crippled by shame.

There was no coming back from this. She wanted to end it all.

————

Sky practically ran into the police station, stumbling over her own feet in her attempts. She burst through the entrance doors and presented herself to an unimpressed desk clerk.

'How can I help?' asked the rotund lady, not moving anything, as if her face and body were frozen. Her upward roll of her eyes to look at Sky screamed dismay and impatience.

'I'm Sky. I'm Ollie's friend. Ollie from last night's hit and run. I found his camera near the scene and there is an image I think you will want to see.'

The desk clerk stared with her deadpan face before very slowly moving out of her seat. 'Wait here. I'll go and get someone.' She couldn't have seemed less interested if she tried, topped with being seemingly irritated by having to leave her desk.

'Top employee you've got there,' whispered Sky to herself.

Half an hour later, Sky was by Ollie's side. The police had taken the camera from her and had thanked her for handing it in. They didn't say what they were going to do or what the current status was, but Sky felt glad that she had been able to help. She had done it for Ollie really, but if that meant getting the correct culprit for this horrific incident, then that was an added bonus.

'I've been to the police station,' she said, rubbing his hair away from his eyes. 'I found your camera. There are some great shots on there, Olz. But it looks like you actually captured the car that hit you moments before. They nicked a girl for it, but your photo shows she wasn't driving. I don't know what will happen next but thank God you took that photo. Now, we just need to get you better and get past what has happened. I love you Ollie, and I'm so sorry about what happened. You're my best friend and I want that to still be the case. Come on, Ollie. Give me something. Flicker your eyes or squeeze my hand. Please.' Sky hung her head at his lack of response.

She looked up again and shook her head at his battered and bruised face and body. His lips were split and swollen. His eyes were swollen and sealed closed. His jaw had been broken too. She squeezed his hand one more time and just as she was about to pull away, she felt his hand move in hers, ever so gently. Her body jolted and she leaned in close to his face.

'Ollie! Are you there? Are you waking up? Oh God, I'm so happy. I was so scared you were gone. Oh God, thank you! Can you squeeze my hand again?'

He did again. It was a very tiny, weak squeeze but it was the biggest feeling of joy for Sky.

'Wait here.' She giggled. 'What did I say that for? You're not going anywhere. I'm going to get a nurse. I'm so fucking happy, Ollie!' She dashed out of the room and went and got the nurse to come and check him over.

———

Curled up in the fetus position, Alice was startled by the rattling of keys at her cell door and dreading what was coming next. She hadn't slept a wink at all that night and had watched the dull cell come to light again as the sun came up and beamed in through the bars of the small window above her bed. She couldn't take much more and wanted to be left alone.

'Out you come. You're going home.' The big burly warden offered her a warm smile.

'What? I ... I don't understand.'

'All will be explained. Come on, there's a cup of tea waiting for you in the interview room.'

His smile felt like a cup of warm sugary tea she thought as her chin began to wobble furiously.

The guard made way for her to exit the cell as she did so, hunched up and tense. She couldn't make any sense of what was happening. There were no thoughts, just a sensation of cotton wool in her head. She pulled out the chair and sat down, as if battered and bruised. The two officers looking at her with small smiles and sympathy in their eyes.

'It's over, Alice. Well, it's not over but we aren't charging you for the hit and run.'

'What? Why?'

'A young woman handed in Ollie's camera to us yesterday afternoon. On it was a picture of you and Phil Evans in the car. Phil was behind the wheel. Phil hit Ollie, Alice.' A huge wave of relief washed over Alice like a tsunami and the tears burst out of her as she sobbed heartily. They pushed a box of tissues towards her and allowed her to grieve for what had been a terrible twenty - four hours. 'There is more, Alice. The swabs came back inconclusive. We believe he assaulted you and attempted worse, but we believe he was not successful in his attempts with you. Now, you've been through a lot, so we are going to take you home and we will come to yours tomorrow and see if we can get any more information from you about what you can remember. But for now, we think you should be at home, with a friend or someone? Get some rest and we will pick this up again when you have slept, ok?' Alice nodded in amongst the sobs.

'I'd like to know who found the camera. I'd like to thank her.'

'Of course. We will pass on your details, and if she wants to make contact, then we will leave that to you both. Alice, we will get justice for you and Ollie and we will get you victim support, ok? Please take care of yourself. Shall we go?'

Alice had begun to control her tears but still needed the occasional gasp of air.

She stared out of the police car window, feeling like her life had been turned upside down. At least she hadn't been driving but she had been raped and that was something she was going to have to come to terms with. It was going to take time.

———

Dear diary,

It's me, Alice. Today was hard, but the chapter is now finally closed. A year since the crash, today the jurors gave a unanimous guilty verdict of causing death by dangerous driving and of sexual assault and attempted rape. He, I can't bring myself to say his name, will be sentenced next week.

I don't know if I could've gotten through it had it not been for Sky, Hannah and Craig. We were all there and held hands as we waited for justice to be served. When the verdict was announced, we hugged and cried together. Meeting Sky, Hannah and Craig has helped me to change my life. Sky lost her best friend, but by finding that camera we found each other. We were there for each other as we grieved. Everyone else tried, but it was heavy, and it was raw. Sky and I understood each other's pain and bonded because of it.

I haven't touched alcohol since I was released. Out of all of this, I found sobriety and I found a new friends in Hannah, Craig, and Sky. Hannah and Craig wanted to make sure that justice was served for Ollie and I'm glad they got in touch because our lives have all improved for it. Hannah has been counselling me through my grief and if it wasn't for Craig, well then, I wouldn't have met Matt.

I wish I had met Ollie when he was alive, Sky still torments herself over his death, but we are all helping her with that. He sounds like a remarkable young man, who really did have a talent for photography. A talent that took his life but spared mine.

After the verdict today, we went for cream tea and Craig and Hannah joined us with their new baby, Henry. We got together to discuss setting up a group where young adults can come and talk about any issues they are having. We just want to create a safe place for people to come and feel wanted. Hannah and Craig have offered to sponsor the group with village hall bookings and refreshments and Craig is thinking about organising adventure camps for the members once we are up and running.

It's so strange. Just over a year ago I was destroying my life with alcohol and felt so alone. I wanted to die. I probably was close to dying. Now, my life is full. We all feel awful that Ollie couldn't be here with us, but because of that night, something amazing happened.

We found each other. We are doing something positive, and we are all alcohol-free.

I can't wait to see where the years ahead take us, but all I know is I am the happiest I have ever been.

It was a close call for me, but I made it out the other side and now I have love in my life and purpose. Life is good.

All my love, Alice.

CHAPTER TWENTY-FOUR

Four years later ...

'Come in, please take a seat.'

Alice watched quietly as the young woman in front of her wouldn't make eye contact and twitched nervously. 'It's ok. Everyone is like this the first time. Just take a moment and take some deep breaths. And, when you're ready, I'd like you to tell me why you are here.' Alice smiled warmly at the woman, her eyes gleaming and sparkling.

'Well ... uh ... I think I am depressed, and I am drinking way too much.'

'Thank you. That's a great start.'

Alice began taking notes as the young woman began pouring out her pain.

'So, same time next week?'

Her patient nodded and wiped away a tear.

'Good and this is all normal. This is the first step. You've done really well, and you should be proud of yourself.' Alice opened the door and let her client leave. 'Sky, give me five minutes and then send my next patient in.'

Sky swung round on her swivel chair and gave Alice a wink. 'Gotcha.'

Alice stood in her office and smoothed down her skirt. She went over to the shelves behind her desk and picked up the framed certificate and looked over it. The sun was beaming through the window and caused a rainbow to appear on the wall and it caught her eye. She knew where it was coming from. She held out her left hand and twiddled with the ring on her engagement finger and smiled. Life was good. Very good.

Dear Diary,

I saw a young woman today in my clinic and she reminded me so much of myself all those years ago. She was broken but not unfixable. It's so hard to believe that I was once like that. Now, the smell of alcohol makes me want to throw up. Four years sober. If only I could tell everyone how much more life has to offer without alcohol. Alcohol is a thief. Alcohol is a very addictive drug and some of us just can't handle it that well. Let there be no shame in that. It's normal to not handle it well. It's poison.

Now that I am sober, I see the world with new eyes. Things are prettier and I generally have a sunnier disposition. Everything feels manageable. I can't believe how much time I have now. I can get so much done in a day. I am not wasting hours trying to black out and then I am not wasting hours recovering. But do you know what? I survived and if going through that meant I could come out the other side and help other people, then the time I wasted was not a waste. I just wish that I had only wasted a fraction of that time, but we know that is not how addiction works.

When I sobered up, I just wanted to shout it out to the world that there is more to life than alcohol. Living with alcohol abuse is no life. It can be so hard when you are stuck in a rut, but what I found is that a problem is nowhere near as much of a problem with a clear head. I used to feel so overwhelmed. I had raging paranoia as if something bad was going to happen at any moment. I lived in fear and bad health. The only way to feel better was to poison myself every night.

I'm not an addiction expert, but I am a counsellor, and I love helping my clients find the answers—and as I always tell them, it is never at the bottom of a bottle.

Love, Alice xx

ABOUT THE AUTHOR

 Lucinda Lamont was born in Aberdeen, Scotland. Her family moved to the South Coast of England when she was a teenager and although she spends most of her time in England, she regularly visits family on the northeast coast of Scotland and Shetland Isles.

Lucinda studied Performing Arts and Law before opting for a career in technology sales for over a decade. She wrote her first book aged twenty-seven and her books have been translated into other languages and are available as Audiobooks.

When not writing, working or running around after her young son, Lucinda enjoys ambling around the Hampshire countryside, looking for ideas for her next story.

—————

To learn more about Lucinda Lamont and discover more Next Chapter authors, visit our website at www.nextchapter.pub.

Dear Diary, It's Me
ISBN: 978-4-82416-872-6
Mass Market

Published by
Next Chapter
2-5-6 SANNO
SANNO BRIDGE
143-0023 Ota-Ku, Tokyo
+818035793528

10th February 2023

www.ingramcontent.com/pod-product-compliance
Lightning Source LLC
LaVergne TN
LVHW031430170726
843492LV00010B/2938